RUTHLESS

Kiss

AMELIA WILDE

DEDICATION

This book is for all my fans who love some sexy power games behind closed doors, and all my fans who inspire me to keep writing. And to my writer friends: I'd be nothing without you!

CONTENTS

CHAPTER ONE

Isabella

"**I** JUST NEED THAT BIG, BEAUTIFUL SIGNATURE OF YOURS ON the dotted line, and these deals are *final*." My lawyer, one Penelope Drake, flips through a few other pages. "And on pages seven, and nine." She sits ramrod straight in the client's seat across my desk from me, her red hair in an impeccable bun at the nape of her neck. Her eyes display only the slightest hint of nervousness.

I'm impressed.

"You had Mark Hudson reevaluate those details?" I pick up the first contract from the top of the pile and scan it one more time.

"Absolutely. The terms now match your exact specifications." I hired Penelope from the newly expanded Grant and Associates to negotiate this expansion, and I have *not* been disappointed.

Juliet Grant might have started out relatively small—at least for New York City—but her firm is a powerhouse now. I took a chance with them, and it's paid off. Women have to stick together.

Especially when men are such unholy assholes.

I keep the scowl off my face and force myself to triple-check the contracts one more time. The last thing on Earth I'm going to do now is let my ex throw me off my game.

He could never play at my level anyway.

Penelope has a better poker face than my financial adviser, Bernadette, who looks like she might stroke out at any moment. She presses her fingertips to her lips. It's not enough to keep the words in.

"Isa, I *have* to remind you—"

"I know, Bernadette."

"It's my *duty* to remind you, one more time, before you sign these, that—"

I fold my hands over the contracts and look across the desk at her. "That this is a short-term risk involving my business capital."

"And personal capital. It's a *massive* risk, Isa. If anything goes wrong—"

"Bernadette," I say, keeping my tone as soothing as possible. Bernadette has been with me since I rented two racks in the corner of a boutique a block down from my shitty studio apartment. I was eighteen. "I love you dearly. But this is a risk I can afford to take."

She takes in one more breath through her nose. "Now. You can afford it *now*."

"I get it, Bernie. I really do."

I pick up a pen on my desk, testing its weight in my hand before I undo the cap. Penelope holds her breath.

I steady myself, check all the small details a final time, then sign my name with a flourish. All nine times.

When I'm finished, Penelope doesn't breathe a sigh of relief—to her credit. She just beams at me across the desk, and even Bernadette gives me a smile. "Congratulations, Isabella." The name still sounds awkward in her mouth, even though I asked her after two weeks to please stop calling me Ms. Gabriel. Most people—at least those who have to hear from me as often as my lawyer does—call me Isa, but I've had no luck convincing her of that.

"On to bigger and better things," I say. We all stand up, and Penelope sweeps the contracts into a file folder and tucks it into the briefcase she always carries with her.

"The new stores will be a hit." She extends her hand across the desk for me to shake. "I'm looking forward to hearing how everything goes."

Buying three storefronts is only the beginning. "Oh, you will," I promise.

Bernadette nods at me, pride shining in her eyes. Once a decision is made, she always gets on board. "Good for you, sweetheart."

She disappears through the door just behind Penelope. I wait until I hear the elevator doors slide closed behind them before I pull the bottle of champagne from my mini-fridge, along with a single fluted glass.

That's all I need.

I let myself grin a little while I pop the cork and pour into the glass, watching the bubbles rise to the surface. This feels amazing. I sure as hell couldn't afford champagne back when I first started this business, borrowing my mother's sewing machine, working in the hallway of the cramped one-bedroom in the Bronx. There wasn't room for the machine and the tiny table it sat on anywhere else in the apartment—not with all three of us sharing the bedroom, my mom and sister in one bed, me in a twin bed, a foot of space the only gap between them.

So Jason was a dick. That doesn't make me want to celebrate less. He almost had me, too—I was ready to put his ring on my finger, so damn head over heels that I almost, *almost,* was willing to marry that bastard without a prenup.

"Be done with him," I command myself. Time to get him out of my head.

I lift the champagne glass and close my eyes. I never thought I'd get this far. I *never* thought I'd be selling my clothes in storefronts all over Manhattan.

And as of today, I'm going statewide.

A thrill goes down my spine, along with yet another jolt of

adrenaline. I'm not about to let Bernadette be right with all her doomsday predictions.

My office seems bathed in a new light when I open my eyes. The clouds that rolled over Manhattan earlier this morning must have cleared. It's too bad. I love a good storm.

I raise my glass, silently toasting the picture of my fourteen-year-old self, hunched over the sewing machine in the light of a single lamp. I'm not looking at the camera. My skinny frame is totally absorbed in the piece I'm sewing. "We've come a long way."

My phone rings, the ringtone loud and insistent, scaring the shit out of me. I was looking forward to the bubbly sweetness of the champagne, the glass halfway to my lips, but it shakes in my hand as I scramble for the phone.

"Isabella Gabriel," I answer. There's a muffled sob from the other end of the line, and my stomach turns over. "Mom?"

"Isa?"

"What's wrong?" I put the champagne flute down on the desk, and it rattles in place. "Mom, talk to me." If she's crying this hard, it has to be terrible news. "Is Evie okay? What's going on?" A thousand possibilities tumble through my mind, each worse than the last. More sobbing. "Mom. *Mom*. Take a deep breath."

She takes a long, shuddering breath. "I got—I got a notice."

What the hell? "What kind of notice? I don't understand, Mom."

"A notice that—that all the leases are being terminated. We're not going to be allowed to renew at the end of August."

"The lease on your apartment?" She's been living in the same building in Hamilton Heights since I was nineteen. There's no way they're kicking her out. "That's not possible."

"It's been bought." A hot spike of anger cuts straight through my gut. There's a crinkle of paper, like she's smoothing it out in her hands. "A developer, I think." She chokes up again. "Isa, everybody has to go. Where am I going to go?"

If I know anything about New York City—and I sure as hell do—then I have a guess as to who's behind this. *Damn it,* that was my next big goal—getting her building under *my* control. *Shit.*

"What developer, Mom? What does it say?"

"Pace, Inc."

I grit my teeth to keep from cursing out loud, upsetting her even more. Those bastards have been buying up every promising property on the island and gutting them for luxury condos, forcing out people—like my mom—every step of the way.

A cold determination fills my chest. Not this time.

"You don't have to worry, Mom. I'm going to take care of this." I get her off the phone with a promise to come for dinner by the end of the week.

My desk chair slides back an inch when I stab the button to turn on my computer monitor.

I'm going straight to the top, and I know exactly who I'm going to confront about this.

All I have to do is find him.

CHAPTER TWO

Jasper

"TO THE PACE EMPIRE!"

My father raises his glass and takes a sip. Everyone clustered around my desk does the same. The tumbler feels heavy, solid in my hand, and the whiskey goes down smooth. It's a Highland Park 30—not nearly the caliber of the Macallan 55 I have in my penthouse, but there's no damn way I'm going to break that out every time we close another deal. Not at the rate I'm going.

When the toast is finished, the guys scatter, heading back to their respective offices. "Find me more buildings!" I call after Mike Ford, the guy who's singlehandedly located at least three diamonds in the rough in the last month alone.

He gives me a jaunty salute from the doorway. "You got it, boss."

My father beams after him, waiting until the last of them are gone before he turns back to me. "Hell of a job, son. Hell of a job."

I sip the last of my whiskey and put the tumbler on the little tray perched on the edge of my desk. "Three more buildings. I wanted five by July."

He laughs. "You've still got time."

Time—but it never feels like I have enough. "Three weeks, two buildings—I'm sure I can pull it off."

"No doubt." Declan Pace's blue eyes, a mirror image of mine, sparkle in the afternoon sunlight pouring in through my office windows. The floor-to-ceiling glass gives me an incredible view of Manhattan. From here, the city looks clean and alive and *close*— close enough for me to reach out and grab with both hands. There's more out there for the taking, and I'm going to find it. "No doubt at all."

I sit back down in the executive chair behind my desk, giving my father a nod. But he doesn't head for the door, back to his own office at the other end of the hallway. "Something on your mind, Dad?"

He considers me, taking another measured sip of his whiskey. "I'm impressed."

"By what?"

"By you. You've got the same kind of killer instinct I had when I started this firm."

I fold my arms over my chest and lean back, smiling at him. "I don't know if I'd think of it as killer. We're *improving* Manhattan one building at a time, even if the riffraff has a problem with it."

Dad laughs out loud. "They're not riffraff, son. They're future tenants."

I wave my hand in the air. "Behind closed doors, I know you agree with me."

He cuts his gaze at my open office door, then gives me a level look. "It's about time you took over the enterprise, Jasper."

I can't help but chuckle at that. "Don't joke around. I've got contracts to sign."

"I'm not joking." His eyes haven't left mine, and there's no trace of a smile on his face now.

I straighten up in my seat. "I see that now, but—"

"What changed my mind?"

"Yes." My dad has lived and breathed Pace, Inc. for thirty years. He's been the first one in the office and the last one out more days than not. What the hell happened to make him want to loosen his grip on his empire?

"Are you telling me you didn't notice that you had more and more to do over the past year?"

"I noticed. I didn't think that meant you were interested in something as absurd as retirement." The image of my father lounging on a white-sand beach somewhere makes a laugh bubble up in my chest. Laying around like some kind of lazy asshole seems antithetical to...well, the rest of his life.

He wags a finger at me, a spark coming back into his eyes. "I didn't say I was going to *retire*."

"But you're ready to be done with Pace, Inc.?" My heart picks up speed. To be in charge, in every way possible—it's so tantalizing I can practically taste it. There's already a low hum of adrenaline racing through my veins. Pace, Inc., *mine*. I could get more aggressive in Paris and London and Dubai. I could own those markets.

"It's pretty clear that you're ready to take matters into your own hands. These last three buildings are a major coup." I get ready to scoff—they're a fantastic deal, but not any more so than the five before—but Dad cuts me off. "You've assembled a damn good team here. You haven't needed me to steer you toward a good find in a year. You don't need me here." He leans in with a conspiratorial grin. "I've got a thirst."

"There's more whiskey." I grin back.

"For new markets."

"You want to expand Pace, Inc. elsewhere? We're worldwide already."

"No, no." He shakes his head, his eyes going distant. "I want to start something, build it from the ground up."

"At sixty-five?" I laugh.

"I've got nothing but time."

"And money."

"That's right." The last of his whiskey gone, he sets the

tumbler next to mine and stands up. "We'll continue this discussion later."

I stand along with him, possibilities thrumming in my veins, and reach out to shake his hand. He looks me square in the eye. "Keep up the good work. Don't ever take your eye off the prize."

"I won't." The prize—money. Power. *Always*.

He goes whistling out the door, and I stand at my desk for a long moment, fingertips pressed against the polished surface, a new fire lit in my gut.

Yes. Today is a good fucking day.

I sit down in my seat, pull the contracts toward me, and scrawl my signature at the bottom of each. "Christine?"

My executive secretary, a willowy blonde who wears her skirt suits like high fashion, is instantly at the doorway. "Yes, Mr. Pace?"

I hold out the papers to her. "Get these down to legal immediately. I want to get started on these buildings as soon as we can." I can't wait to have my driver take us past, watch the rotted innards of these properties hauled out to make room for gleaming interiors, for shining lobbies, all the old stripped away to reveal the true potential of the place.

She nods and glides gracefully back out the door. I know exactly how long it takes to get down to legal, so it should be no longer than fifteen minutes before my phone rings, and—

Christine's voice rises outside the door. "No, I'm sorry, miss. Mr. Pace doesn't allow unscheduled appointments." *What the hell?*

"That's *Ms.* Gabriel. And he'll make an exception for me." The low voice is commanding and leaves no room for argument. A crackling curiosity short-circuits my focus on the new buildings. Who in this city has the balls to interrupt my afternoon without an appointment?

There's a long pause. "That's simply not—wait. Ms. Gabriel—"

Then she's standing in the doorway, fire in her eyes, a glare that sends a spike of heat straight down my spine. Christine hovers behind her, but doesn't dare get too close. When she speaks, her voice is razor-sharp. "So *you're* the bastard who's ruining my day."

CHAPTER THREE

Isabella

J ASPER PACE IS DEFINITELY NOT THE OLDER MAN I'VE SEEN IN the papers representing this evil empire of a company. In fact, he's not an older man at all.

He's young, and he's hot as *hell.*

When he stands up from behind his desk, I get an eyeful of an expensive suit so closely tailored to his body that it doesn't leave much to the imagination.

Under any other circumstance, I'd be into the view, because Jasper Pace—that's the name on the office door—is a living Greek statue, all hard muscle and chiseled jaw. And those eyes—a vivid blue that makes me want to get closer, much closer, just so I can stare into them—send an electric charge tripping down my spine straight between my legs.

That doesn't make him any less of a scumbag.

An amused grin plays over his face, and I hate him a little more. "I don't think we've met. I'm Jasper Pace." His secretary is practically breathing down my neck. I wish she'd sit down in her pretty little suit and let me take care of business. Jasper looks past me. "We're all right, Christine."

She sniffs, and I keep my eyes locked on Jasper's face while she walks away. He's not going to throw me off my game with his slick, charming manners. Screw that.

"No, we *haven't* met, but that hasn't stopped you from turning a great day into a shitty one."

His eyebrows go up an inch, but the smile stays in place. "Why don't you have a seat?" There are two leather armchairs in front of his massive mahogany desk. I'm sure that's where people come to sell their damn souls along with their real estate.

"I'd rather not."

He shrugs, and even the shrug reeks of all the power he thinks he has. He might be one of the billionaires of Pace, Inc., but he doesn't know me. If I'd met him a week ago, I might have been impressed. Now, the sight of him has rage boiling over in my gut...and a heat between my legs, but I'll be damned if I'll admit that. "Your choice. You could at least come in, though. I have a feeling you might want this conversation to be private."

"I don't give a damn who hears."

His grin gets wider, and he moves out from behind his desk. "All right. Well, *I'd* prefer if we kept things to ourselves." He strides across the office and steps into the doorway, leaning close so that he can reach for the open door's handle. I can't help but inhale his scent, and damn it, he smells good—like the kind of cologne you have personally made, underneath a pure clean scent that clings to his skin. "If you'll excuse me—Ms. Gabriel, wasn't it?"

I stand my ground, glaring at him from close range, but he doesn't falter, that infuriating smile still wrinkling the corners of his eyes. My heart beats hard against my ribs, the tension going taut in the air between us.

This is ridiculous. There are bigger battles to be won.

I step into the office. Jasper pulls the door closed, then moves a few steps back toward his desk, crossing his arms over his chest. "Enlighten me. What exactly have I done to ruin your day?"

I grit my teeth to keep from slapping him. Or kissing him. The urge comes over me so strongly that it's all I can do to stay in place. *What the hell, Isa?* Looking into the face of my mortal enemy shouldn't be turning me on, but it is.

Focus.

"Well, Mr. *Pace,* I think you've gone far enough with your reckless destruction of the city."

He raises one eyebrow. "Reckless?"

"Arrogant. Greedy. Rushed. These are all words I'd use to describe the way you and your company have been gutting buildings and shattering communities from the East Village to Harlem." I shake my head in disgust. "When is enough going to be enough for you people?"

He considers me, his smile turning sly, and now he's close

enough for me to see that his eyes are blue with a shock of silver around the pupils. They're breathtaking. Their only competition is from...the rest of his body. "One thing you should know about me, Ms. Gabriel, is that enough is never enough." He shifts his weight, and his tailored suit displays a whole new dimension of his physique. His eyes burn into mine. "The other thing you should know is that I disagree with your assessment."

"I'm shocked," I deadpan.

He goes on as if he hasn't heard me. "This firm doesn't *shatter* communities. It improves them. We're taking buildings that are out of date, most of them with serious infrastructure issues, and turning them into homes that anyone would be proud to live in." He cocks his head to the side. "I can't see how you'd have a problem with that."

"It's not improvement I have a problem with." My face is hot with anger, and my hands tremble at my sides. "But you're only in it for the money, clearly."

"It *is* an incredible side bonus."

I hate him, but more than that, I hate my own body for wanting him so badly, in this moment of all moments.

I narrow my eyes. "I should have known this would be a pointless discussion." I can't keep my mouth from curling into a sneer. "I'll be sure to explain to my mother—who's losing her home because of you, by the way—that at least you're getting an *incredible side bonus.*"

Before he can say another word, I turn on my heel and head

for the door. My hand is on the handle, my muscles tensed to push it open, when— "Wait."

"What?" I spit the word over my shoulder.

"I didn't realize you were here to discuss a personal issue." His tone is mild, but when I turn back around, his gaze is electric. "That changes everything."

CHAPTER FOUR

Jasper

"**D**OES IT?" MS. GABRIEL TURNS BACK, DROPPING HER HAND away from the handle and facing me head on. "Why am I not surprised?"

"I'm not in the business of ruining lives, Ms. Gabriel. If I'd known you were coming in to negotiate some kind of lease, we could have started there. Or I could have directed you to the appropriate department."

She gives me an exasperated half-smile. "I find it's more effective to start at the source of the problem." *Damn.* This woman fears absolutely nothing. The more she says, the more I want her.

It makes no sense whatsoever, that this hurricane of a woman should interest me at all. She's exactly the kind of distraction my father warned me about fifteen years ago, after his last romantic entanglement went sour. He'd come home in the middle of the night reeking of the bar, causing such a commotion in the entryway of the condo in Midtown we were living in that I disengaged myself from the date I'd brought home—a redhead, I can't remember her name—and gone to see what the fuss was about. He'd grabbed the front of my shirt in both fists. "It's not worth it. It's never worth it, son. Focus on getting ahead." Then he'd stumbled into his bedroom and shut the door, not coming out for two days.

My cock is painfully hard against the fabric of my pants. As casually as I can, I move back behind my desk and take a seat. "I'm assuming this has to do with one of the properties I recently acquired."

Isabella's eyes, green like the jungle, green like the leaves that surround a panther about to pounce, follow my every movement. She bites her lip, then seems to make a decision. She moves across the office, her hips swaying underneath a black skirt suit that hugs her curves. Every movement sends fire through my chest. I want to bend her over the desk, shove her skirt up around her hips, and teach her a lesson or two about how to be polite. The confidence radiating off of her tells me that she'd be absolutely filthy in bed. Or on the floor. Or on her knees, right here in my office. I'd love to fist her long, dark hair in my hands until it's a rumpled mess, far from the perfect state it's currently in.

She takes a seat, back perfectly straight. "Does Hamilton Heights ring any bells to you, Mr. Pace?" Her tone drips with sarcasm, like I couldn't possibly remember one building out of the tens of buildings I've "destroyed" throughout Manhattan. If only she knew…

I smile at her like she's the most important partner I've ever met with. "Of course. Eight stories, currently a walk-up. Needs significant renovation, but there's room for sixteen luxury condos, plus accessibility features. At *least* one elevator."

Her cheeks go a little pink. *Bet you weren't expecting that.* I don't fool around with my business. I make it a point to know everything I can about every one of my properties. I'm sure all the other real estate moguls she knows take a different approach.

"And a man like you, with a company like yours, probably has buyers lined up for each and every one of those already."

"I'm holding a couple in reserve."

"That's so kind."

I lean toward her, folding my arms on the surface of the desk. "This isn't about luxury condos, though, is it, Ms. Gabriel? This is about your mother. I'm not sure what that would have to do with the Hamilton Heights property, however. It's unoccupied."

"It's *not* unoccupied." Her eyes narrow, her mouth pressed into a thin line, and her expression—hard and fierce and unrelenting—makes my cock twitch in my pants. "It will *be* unoccupied once you're finished forcing out all the current tenants."

An alarm is ringing in the back of my mind. A man's voice on the other end of the line: *"Every single one of them, unoccupied. Sitting there, empty space."* He'd laughed, a deep rumble. *"It's best for everyone if you take it off my hands. I'm done with it. I'm done."*

Clearly, that's not the case.

Ms. Gabriel goes on. "The building was one of the last in the neighborhood with rent-controlled spaces, so you can imagine how it felt to receive notice today that none other than Pace, Inc. has decided not to let any of the tenants renew their leases. Such a nice way to end a tenant relationship that's lasted a decade." Her expression is somewhere between a smirk and a scowl.

I'm torn neatly in two. The half of me that's interested in peeling those clothes away from her body until there's nothing between her flawless skin and the cool air of my office, watching her nipples pebble away from the swell of her breasts, putting my hands all over her, is insisting that I back down. I could smooth this over. I could tell her that this is all a misunderstanding—that in fact, the rarest occasion is happening right now. I was misled, and there was no follow-up. Someone at Pace, Inc. is going to be fired over this, that's for damn sure.

The other half of me is rising to the bait of her sneer. Nobody talks to me that way—not anymore. I'm the one who sits in the driver's seat, and Ms. Gabriel is a guest in my office. She's not a client, even if she's sitting in the client's seat.

I'm not backing down.

I fold my hands on the desk and meet her gaze without flinching. "I'm sorry to hear that your mother was upset." I keep my voice even. "It's...unfortunate when residents have to be relocated, but the neighborhood will benefit in the long term." I give her a big, wide smile. "Who knows? Your mother may even want to purchase one of the condos I'm holding in reserve. I'd be happy to hold one for her, if she'd like to come in and take a look at the floor plans."

Her hands tighten on the arms of the chair, and the blush on her face deepens. She takes a long breath in through her nose, then inhales slowly out of her perfect lips. I'd like to see those lips, in that exact shade of red lipstick, wrapped around something more substantial than air.

I get ready for Ms. Gabriel to stand up and head for the door. I've made it abundantly clear that strolling into my office like this isn't going to get her anywhere.

What happens next, I don't see coming.

A slow smile spreads across her face, and then she chuckles, a sound low in her chest. "You know something, Mr. Pace?" Her breasts rise and fall underneath the silk shell she's wearing beneath her blazer. "I think we got off on the wrong foot. I think..." Her voice trails off, and her green eyes linger on my face. "I think that if we try—if we really try—we could work this out."

CHAPTER FIVE

Isabella

E VERY WORD OUT OF HIS MOUTH IS A TAUNT, A TEASE...AN invitation. I can't ignore the way his voice sends tendrils of pure desire curling down my spine.

I also can't ignore the fact that he's being an unbelievable asshole about this.

Then there's the other problem party in this discussion: yours truly. My mother's voice echoes in my head, some old bullshit truism about catching more flies with honey. I should have centered myself on that before I charged up here.

The comment about my mother buying one of his luxury condos, though—that was the last straw.

I throw down the gauntlet, my words landing squarely in the air between us, and put on my very best apologetic-yet-sensual face. I watch the words register. I watch the look in eyes go from a ruthless determination to curiosity to something that looks suspiciously like need. Everything flashes through his expression in a matter of seconds, and then he shakes his head. "I don't know about that, Ms.—"

I hold up both hands. "Let's back up. Partners in such an—" I bite my lip, "—*intimate* discussion should be on a first-name basis." I extend one hand toward him, feeling another inch of air on my cleavage as I lean forward. "I'm Isabella Gabriel."

He flicks his gaze to my hand, then reaches out for it. At the touch of his palm against mine my entire body thrills, my nipples going hard against the lacy fabric of my bra. Damn Jasper Pace for being so hot. Damn him.

"Jasper Pace," he says, his firm grip lasting a second too long on mine. "But you already knew that."

I sit back in my seat, raising a hand to my hair. "On some level, I guess." I give him a rueful smile. "I thought you were going to be...you know, older."

He laughs out loud, an easy laugh that untwists some of the anger knotted in my gut. "You probably meant to speak to my father, Declan Pace." I roll my eyes a little—*of* course *I did.* "Better me than him. I don't think he would appreciate being called a greedy bastard in his own office."

I bite back the urge to tell him that his father would deserve the title. I take another breath in and tilt my head down, looking at Jasper from underneath my eyelashes. "I didn't come here intending to say those things."

"What did you intend to do?" Jasper's blue eyes, the silver ring around his pupils catching the light streaming in through the ostentatiously huge windows lining two corners, burn into mine, suspicion and delight battling there. He probably feels pretty damn superior, now that I'm backed into a corner.

And I'll never admit it. I'll never admit to anyone the way my heart is pounding, the way my stomach is knotting up again, because all this—all the angry words I've spit at him, all the fire in my chest, still won't be enough if I can't convince him to let my mother stay in her apartment. I took three more panicked phone calls on the way over, each worse than the last.

I never should have signed those contracts. If I'd just been more sensible about it, I would have just enough capital to negotiate with him on the level of the building. But I don't. It's all tied up in my own ambition.

I swallow hard, and it's not just for show. The rage that fueled my trip to Jasper's Midtown offices can't keep up with the heart-thudding attraction I'm fighting off right this very minute or the sickening guilt that rears its head every time the sound of my mother's sobs creeps back into my head.

The grand ideas I had about negotiating with him on a financial level collapse under the weight of his gaze. What was I thinking, coming here like this, unprepared and upset? He's so smug. I shouldn't want to look at his face, much less the rest of him.

Why do I want to keep my eyes on his for the rest of the day? Maybe the rest of the *week*?

Get. A. Grip, Isa.

Jasper Pace is just like every other man in Manhattan—arrogant, self-absorbed, and entirely unworthy of my emotions. He and Jason would have a lot to talk about. Jason's confession is still ringing in my ears. *She's just someone I couldn't let go of,* he'd said, trying his level best to look contrite. *I know it was wrong. I never meant to hurt you.*

Who the hell knows? Maybe Jason was just too stupid to realize he'd ever get caught out with a second girlfriend. But Jasper? Jasper delights in making me squirm. I can see it on his face.

What he doesn't know—what men like Jasper Pace never know—is that he's not the only one who can play this game.

It comes to me in a flash. I don't have any money to bargain with. All I have is the strange, heavy heat that hangs in the air between us. He knows how hot he is. He knows what effect he must have on most women.

He's no match for me.

He's no match for me—but I'm going to make him think that he is.

I bite my lip and look into his eyes like I'm seeing them for the first time. "I came here hoping to make a deal."

"A deal? What kind of deal? The building is mine, Isabella."

"I know." I let my voice drop, sultry and smooth. "You have all the cards." I press my lips together. "I just want one of them. My mother—" I press my fingertips to my lips, shaking my head a little. "She worked all her life to move into that apartment. She's prided herself on never missing a rent payment since she moved in. It's everything to her."

Jasper takes in a breath, leaning in, just a little. He thinks I didn't notice the bulge in the front of his pants before he sat down. And I've got him now. I've almost got him.

Time to land this.

I put both hands on the very edge of his desk, my grip light, like I might need to grab on for dear life at any moment. "I'll do anything, Jasper. Just—please, let her stay. *Anything*."

CHAPTER SIX

Jasper

I can't read the look on Isabella's face, but her name echoes in my mind. I want to taste it on my tongue. I want to taste *her* on my tongue. And I don't trust this shift in tactics. Five minutes ago, she was calling me a bastard from the doorway of my own office and looked ready to tear me into a thousand pieces.

The heat isn't gone from her face. If anything, it's almost intensified—but the words dripping from her lips are a breath away from begging, and it's the most beautiful sound in the world. *I'll do anything, Jasper. Anything.*

It's only a shadow of how she'd sound if she was moaning my name, pleading for the kind of sweet release I'd play out for minutes—hours, if necessary. Her green eyes are wide, breasts lifting underneath the thin silk shell, and those lips—Jesus, those lips—parted while she waits for me to answer...

Isabella Gabriel is playing a dangerous game.

Can it really be all about her mother's apartment?

It hardly matters to me whether the woman wants to move or not. If she wants to stay in the building badly enough, she'll come up with the funds to buy one of the renovated condos. Hell, if it resolves the slight issue of the seller lying through his teeth to not only me, but Mike Ford, and who knows who else at Pace, Inc., it might be worth the cost.

I'm not going to say that to Isabella.

Not yet.

I'm going to keep my cards face down on the table. She might have her most contrite face on right now, but I saw her when she came in. I'm not as witless as she thinks I am.

I could dismiss her right now, and show her who's really in charge.

Or I could let her dangle for a little while longer. I could buy some time to decide what to do.

I choose door number two.

"Anything?" I let the word roll off my tongue, narrowing my eyes. Isabella's fingertips rest lightly on the edge of my desk, but her grip tightens at the word. An image flashes into my mind—her bent over this desk, knuckles white while she holds on for dear life. And me? God, the options would be endless. I could bring my palm down against her creamy, flawless ass. I could work my fingers between her legs, teasing at her clit, making her spread those legs wider and wider until she can't buck against my fingers, until she'd have to let me take total control if she wanted to get off.

Her tongue darts between her lips, but she doesn't take her eyes off mine. "*Anything.*"

I lean back in my seat, linking my hands together behind my head. "It seems odd," I say casually, "that five minutes ago you were ready to tear me limb from limb, and now you're ready to give away...anything."

"My mother—"

"I'm not sure you've quite thought through the consequences of a word like anything, Isabella." I was right. Even her name feels sweet in my mouth, even if a wayward breeze could have her shooting daggers at me with her eyes.

She straightens up again, putting her hands in her lap. "That's where you're wrong, Jasper."

"About which thing? Tearing me apart?"

Isabella bites her lip. "Both. I was—" Her eyes dart down to her lap, then back to my face. "I was upset. I was angry. If you only knew how much that apartment means to my mother—" She breaks off. "That doesn't matter. That's personal. This is business. I've thought about it, and I will do *anything* to convince you to let her stay."

I grin at her across the desk, leaning forward to pull a folder from one of the drawers. "If you're serious, then there should be a relatively simple solution to all of this."

Isabella can't disguise the hope in her face. "What's that?"

I pull out the packet of papers about the Hamilton Heights building—the outlines of the deal I made to buy it two months ago. It was finalized just last week. The owner clearly didn't waste any time in notifying the tenants, who aren't supposed to exist.

I slide the packet across the desk toward Isabella, and then tap one finger against the sum at the bottom. "Buy it yourself. All you'd have to do is make it worth my while."

Isabella's shoulders sag just a fraction of an inch, and then her guard is back in place. A new flush comes to her cheeks. "If this were any other day—" She lifts the papers from the desk, holding them lightly in her hands, and shakes her head.

"Then what?"

The packet flutters back down to the surface of the desk. "Are we being honest with each other?"

"What else would we be?"

She gives me a wry grin. "Three weeks ago, I could have bought this building from you and had capital left to spare."

"And here I had the impression that you weren't a wealthy woman."

"I do well for myself."

"What business are you in?"

"I'm sure you haven't heard of me. I run a little company called Gabriel Luxe."

It clicks into place then—the fearless attitude, the way she waltzed in here as if she owned the place. She's *the* Isabella

Gabriel, and her fashion company is so buzzy that I've even heard of it at cocktail parties. I laugh out loud. "You're playing with me, Isabella. You're the talk of the city. You're telling me you can't afford this single building? I haven't even started the renovations yet—it's at a rock-bottom price."

There's no hint of embarrassment in her reply. "I'm in the middle of expanding to statewide distribution, with plans to go national by the middle of next year."

Oh. "And you've found yourself a bit...over-leveraged."

"A bit." Another deep breath, and a charge flashes through her eyes. "So I can't deal on financial terms."

My cock is so hard I feel every heartbeat resonating through it. There's no way she's suggesting what I think she's suggesting. There's no way a woman like Isabella Gabriel would ever put herself in that position. And along with the hot, pulsing lust that's echoing through every one of my cells, there's a bright glee. This game is about to get interesting, because she's given me the chance I've been waiting for since she said she'd do...anything.

The chance to call her bluff.

"If finances are off the table..." She waits, her full lips pressed together. I nod, just once, like I've made up my mind once and for all. "I'll accept a different kind of trade. You agree to let me possess you—possess *all* of you—for one month, and I won't force your poor mother to abandon the only home she's ever loved."

"All of me?" The words are low, her eyes wide, cheeks a scarlet red.

"*All* of you. Everything at my discretion. Everything under my control."

It's an outrageous demand, and it's going to send her running for the door.

She sucks in her breath.

CHAPTER SEVEN

Isabella

J ASPER PACE IS ONE BALLSY BASTARD.

I expected some kind of sexual arrangement—I am, after all, leaning slightly forward and breathing just heavily enough to make sure he definitely notices my cleavage—but a *month*? By the way the he phrases "all of you" and "under my control," I'm guessing he's no stranger to the kind of kinky bedroom stuff he has to be alluding to.

What I didn't expect is a hot wetness between my legs, a rush of crackling desire—deeper and darker—through my chest.

But I can't let that get the better of me. This battle of wills with Jasper is going to end with me on top...even if I have to get dirty in the fight.

His blue eyes dance, heat raging there. *He's not expecting me to agree.*

I know it's true as soon as the thought occurs to me. That's the last thing Jasper would anticipate. He's probably waiting for me to slap him across the face right now and storm out, leaving him to bask in yet another triumph.

Not a chance in hell.

I glance down at my hands, letting the moment linger, then I look back up into his laughing gaze. "A month."

It's not really a question, but Jasper nods solemnly. He can't quite keep the smirk off of his face. I swear, if it wouldn't give him away, he'd be rubbing his palms together right now, salivating at the thought of getting the best of me.

I'll give him the best of me. And I'll use it to come out ahead. Way, *way* ahead. He'll never see it coming.

"One month. Non-negotiable."

"I accept."

I say the words like I'd say "no, thank you" to a cashier offering me a plastic bag, and it has exactly the effect I wanted. Jasper's smile stretches even wider, but then it hits him.

His jaw doesn't drop open. He looks me dead in the eye, the strange silver ring around his pupils reflecting the sunlight back into mine. "You accept."

I nod firmly, not dropping my gaze for an instant. "I do."

My heart pounds against my rib cage, beating so hard I'm surprised it doesn't drown out the entire conversation. I'm surprised Jasper hasn't mentioned it. Electricity pulses in my veins, and it's pure torture to have to sit in this chair, my head held high, pretending this is a business transaction and nothing more.

Jasper has to know it's not just a business transaction. He has to know it as well as I know it, from the way he's looking at me. But I'm not going to be the first one to crack, and if this conversation has told me anything about him, he's not going to go down easily.

"You accept all the terms?"

I pitch my voice a little lower. "All of me. Under your control. For one month. Those terms?"

"Yes."

The heat in my chest increases with every breath, a fiery kind of tension that seems to pull me closer to him, even though I don't dare move a muscle in his direction. Jasper's chiseled features could be something out of a movie, out of a fashion magazine, but he's solid and real in a way that the hottest actor could never be. My nipples rub against my bra every time I take air into my lungs.

I don't know if this is my first victory over Jasper or my first loss, but the adrenaline rush makes it feel like a win. I've got him exactly where I want him—at least, I think I do.

"Let me be absolutely clear, Isabella." He leans forward, his expression deadly serious. "When I say *all of you*, I don't mean in a...professional capacity. We might agree to terms that will affect the business relationship we're about to enter into about the Hamilton Heights building, but—"

"You mean all of me. You mean every inch of my body. You

mean—" The kinds of things I've seen in the movies and read in books, and if I'm being honest, the kinds of things I fantasize about more often than not. A powerful man holding me in place, stroking between my legs until I come, helpless and possessed. The crack of a hand against the flesh of my ass, sending a painful pleasure rocketing through my body. *That's* a game I can play.

And if it means playing *him* so that I can keep my mother happy while I figure out an alternate plan to buy her building—further negotiations with Jasper Pace and all—I'll do it.

"I mean submission." He shakes his head a little, his eyes flicking over my breasts and back up to my face. "I mean that I'm going to require a certain level of submission from you, Isabella." He draws in a deep breath. "If that's not something you can handle, you should make that known now."

I'm still spinning my web when I speak again, even if the excitement is building in my gut. *This is a game. This is just a game, and you are playing a part. Play the damn part so well he doesn't know you're acting.* "What makes you think I can't handle you?"

He laughs. "Not a thing." Jasper opens his mouth like he's about to admit something, but thinks better of it. "Are there any details you wanted to discuss today?"

"There is one thing." I'm slated for a million appointments, a million meetings, over the next week. I'm willing to go all in on this—whatever this is, but I have no idea how much time this is going to take. "I need one week."

"A week for what?"

"To...prepare. I didn't expect—" I let the barest hint of a shy smile slide onto my face. "I didn't expect to make this kind of agreement with you when I walked in here today." I take in a breath, blowing it out through my lips like I'm trying to rid myself of quaking nerves. Well, maybe I am, but it's not because I'm afraid of Jasper. I don't know what the hell it is, exactly, that has me feeling so giddy—this asshole deserves everything he's going to get, but even the prospect of revenge isn't enough to explain this thrill.

"Stand up."

The command in his voice takes me off guard, and just like that, every muscle is tensed, my eyes locked on his.

"What?"

"I'll give you your week. We'll begin next Friday."

"Yes. I—" I break off when Jasper stands up from his seat, coming quickly around the desk, to a position so close to my chair that when I do stand he's only inches away. I get another lungful of his scent, and more wetness collects between my legs. He's radiating electricity, radiating power, and I want him.

"This is your last chance to back out." He puts two fingers under my chin and lifts it another inch, forcing me to keep my eyes on his—as if I could bring myself to look away. "Right now."

I narrow my eyes, my breaths shallow. There's not enough air in the room. "I'm *not* backing out."

Then he's leaning toward me, and I'm falling into his orbit, the gravity between us finally overpowering my resistance. My body strains toward him—kiss me, *kiss* me, do it...

There's a knock on the door, knuckles on the solid wood, and Jasper freezes.

CHAPTER EIGHT

Jasper

*I*ALMOST KISSED HER IN MY OFFICE.

My feet connect lightly with the surface of the treadmill in my personal gym. I converted one of the guest bedroom suites into a fully appointed workout room a year ago, but I don't normally spend time here. There's a private fitness center on the second floor that I prefer.

That I *usually* prefer. I've spent so much time exercising this weekend that the trip downstairs, even by private elevator, seems like an unnecessary hassle.

I'm out of ideas. I can't get her out of my mind. Those curves under that skirt suit, those eyes gleaming from her flawless face—they've flashed into my thoughts over and over again from the moment she walked out of my office until now.

I almost kissed her.

I might be the next in line to assume complete ownership of Pace, Inc., but that doesn't absolve me of the kind of trouble that would ensue if Christine walked in on me with my tongue buried in a woman's mouth—especially if that woman is one I might ultimately be making a business deal with.

Not that that stops me from wanting to bend her over that desk, Christine be damned.

I almost lost control. That's the part that shakes me the most. Isabella Gabriel's eyes, her lips, the way she was practically on her knees begging me for a way out of her dilemma—all of it combined to intoxicate me, to overwhelm me.

An evening's worth of drinks with Dominic Wilder and company didn't clear my head. I have a standing arrangement with him and a few other guys who take business seriously. Once a month, we get together. When the first round comes out, we talk strategy, acquisitions, plans. Once the second round is served, all business talk is off limits.

Isabella Gabriel's name was on the tip of my tongue all Friday evening. None of the women fluttering around the table in their too-short dresses and makeup designed to entice made an impression. I opened my mouth to mention her, but every time, the words caught in my throat.

Why?

I bump up the speed on the treadmill, my lungs burning with the effort.

Why couldn't I mention her?

Why is she so impossible to stop thinking of?

I run for another mile, then slap my hand down on the stop bar.

Weights. I need weights. I choose a set that's almost too heavy and force myself through a full circuit, my muscles growing more fatigued with every second that passes by.

A weekend of this. Weights. Treadmills. Round after round of drinks. Sunday afternoon, and I'm considering going into the office, finding something to do...but sitting behind my desk will only make me think of her, her fingertips against the shining surface...

I throw the weights back into the rack and thunder through my penthouse. The staff have the day off, so I'm completely alone.

There's only one more option, and I've been keeping it at arm's length since Friday afternoon, when Isabella Gabriel waltzed into my office and took over my brain.

In the shower, I turn the water on hot and let it cascade down over my shoulders and back—anything to delay taking the next step with this. I don't want her to know how much she's already consumed me, but I'm not in the mood to call anyone from Dominic's group and plan another outing. I also can't sit around in the penthouse all evening, my phone—and my last resort—burning a hole in my consciousness.

Fuck it.

I step out, towel off, pull an outfit from my closet—sweatpants and a soft t-shirt. I'm not going out again. I'm definitely not going to try to run into Isabella. The city is too big for that kind of goose chase, and without knowing her plans...

Which I have no reason to know. Not for another week.

In my living room, I sit back on the cool leather cushions on the sofa, phone in one hand, glossy business card in the other.

Before the door to my office was finished swinging open, Christine interrupting the most charged moment of my entire life and the impulsive kiss I was going for, Isabella had straightened up, pulling herself just far enough out of my grasp that I'm almost certain Christine didn't see anything. Then, a little smile playing over her lips, she'd reached into her purse.

"Here's my contact information, Mr. Pace," she said, as if we were concluding a run-of-the-mill business interaction, as if the little standoff she'd had with Christine had never happened at all. Her eyes flashed, lingering on mine, but her voice gave nothing away. "Stay in touch."

I'd taken the card between my fingers and slipped it into my pocket, nodding at her with the kind of professional smile I'd use to dismiss someone from my office. A slight raise of her eyebrows, just for me, and then Isabella was heading for the door, stepping neatly around Christine, leaving me there with an enormous bulge in my pants and a whirlwind in my mind.

The card has her name printed in bold letters. Underneath, it reads "Founder and CEO, Gabriel Luxe." Across the bottom are two phone numbers, office and cell.

I punch the cell number into my phone, saving it as a contact, and then I bring up a text message. Calling her will seem too desperate, and I'm not willing to give her that satisfaction. Other satisfactions, yes. Knowing that she's taken over my thoughts all weekend, no.

I type out *I've been thinking of next Friday* and delete all of it. What the hell am I thinking?

Start over.

What's your dress size?

I laugh and stab my thumb against the screen, sending the message before I can think about it anymore. That will have her wondering. That will have her staring at her phone somewhere in Manhattan and imagining exactly what I'm planning.

The answer comes back almost immediately.

Who's this? I don't give out my measurements to strangers.

Did I—did I *not* give her my phone number in the office? No. Of course I didn't. Jesus.

You don't recognize my number?

Good save.

There's a longer pause.

I should have known it was you.

Then she doesn't say anything. A minute ticks by, then two.

She's toying with me.

I sit there with the phone in my hands, my thumbs hovering over the screen. Wait thirty seconds more. Another thirty...*do* not *send her another message*.

I'm on the verge of giving in when another message arrives.

Four.

Victory.

CHAPTER NINE

Isabella

"I JUST DON'T KNOW WHERE I'D FIT A THING LIKE THIS." My mom eyes her KitchenAid stand mixer—red, just like she wanted—and wrings her hands.

I drop my phone back into my purse. "It fits right there."

She turns her dark eyes on me, then looks back to the mixer. "In a different apartment."

"First of all..." Was that my phone buzzing in my purse that I just felt, or something else? Another phantom text? I can hardly stop checking the damn thing, now that Jasper has made it clear that he might text me at any time. I reach back down into my purse and pull it out, setting it on the countertop. There's no new message. "First of all, Mom, I'm taking care of it. You don't have to worry about moving into another apartment. And second—"

The phone finally vibrates against the countertop, and I snatch it up.

It's from Angelique, my executive secretary.

I should not feel this disappointed. This is getting ridiculous.

A weekend of feeling hot and bothered, no matter how much I threw myself into drafting distribution plans for the new locations, researching new fabrics for next year's lines, and triple-checking the details on the new locations. I dragged my best friend Charlotte—ever-patient Charlotte—out on a spa day for most of Saturday afternoon.

None of it—none of it *at all*—could keep Jasper Pace out of my head. The kiss that almost was is becoming an instrument of torture, and he didn't even seal the deal. If his uptight secretary hadn't walked in at just that moment...

I should be thanking her. I was just about ready to let Jasper have his way with me, right there in the office. Why does back-and-forth with a powerful man have that effect on me?

It's lingering as hell, too. Right now, I want to walk out the door of my mom's building, hail a cab, and tell the driver to break every traffic law he needs to to get me back to my own place, where I could slip between the sheets with my vibrator and...

"You seem distracted, Isa."

I put the phone back on the countertop a little harder than necessary. "It's just the office checking in."

My mom waves her hands in the air. "You should get back there. I'll be fine."

"You didn't seem fine when you called an hour ago."

"I'm just not sure where I'll put all my things."

I take a deep breath. It's understandable, the way she's reacting. My mom just retired from her full-time job as a schoolteacher last summer, and she's happily settled into a job at the local library branch around the corner. Moving was the last thing on her mind until Friday. "I swear to you, Mom, I'm handling this. You're not going to have to go anywhere."

"Mrs. Callahan broke her lease."

Mrs. Callahan, the ancient woman from across the hall, who was here when she first moved in. "Mrs. Callahan is ninety years old. It makes sense for her to be moving into somewhere with people who can help her day to day. That can't be related to the sale of the building."

There's a rattle of keys in the front door, and then it swings open, banging against the doorstop. "I can't believe it." My sister is a high-fashion tornado, all plum lips and pissed-off eyes. "Why did you wait so long to tell me?" She tosses her purse onto the table in the entryway and stalks into the kitchen on high heels. "They're cancelling all the leases? God, Isa. You should have called me! Mom, I can't believe—"

"I was going to." Mom straightens her back. "I didn't want to upset you."

"What are we going to do about this?" Evie is tall, with my mom's dark eyes instead of the green ones I inherited from the father who jumped ship when I was three and she was one. "There has to be something we can do."

"I'm taking care of it," I say again.

She fixes her gaze on me, cocking her hip to the side. "Are you buying the building?"

"Not yet, but that's in the works."

My mom's mouth drops open. "Oh, Isa, how are you ever going to be able to do that? There's not enough money to outbid someone like Pace, Inc. And if the deal is already final, then that means—"

"Yeah. If the deal is already final, how are you going to step in?" Evie laughs. "Unless you have some *special relationship* with Pace, Inc."

Heat rushes to my cheeks. Where the hell did that come from? Evie doesn't know the first thing about what happened when I went to meet with Jasper.

But she does know me.

"Oh, my god." Her face fills with glee. "You *do* have something going on with that company. Only—no. I bet it's not with the company. I bet it's with Jasper Pace."

I roll my eyes harder than I really need to. "I do *not* have a special relationship with Jasper Pace. Trust me." I don't. I really don't. But his name on my tongue feels sultry in a way that has me on fire, standing here in the middle of my mother's kitchen.

"Tell us, Isa. Are you sleeping with him?"

Not yet. "Mom, are you okay?" I swivel my entire body toward her, avoiding Evie's gaze. "If everything's fine here, I should really get back to the office."

My mom looks at Evie. "Can you stay for dinner?"

"Sure." Evie answers, but she doesn't look away from me.

"Isa?"

"I can't." I can't because I have work to do, and also because if I can't get off within the next hour, I'm going to spontaneously combust. I've tried my best all damn day to keep my mind off Jasper's eyes, off Jasper's body, off Jasper's hands digging into my hips and…

And I can't do it.

I don't want this to rule me. I don't want to have to have the cab drive me back home before I head back to the office.

I'm not sure I have any choice.

"All right." My mom nods, but then her hand rises to her throat and she sniffs. Evie shoots me a glare and goes to wrap her arm around Mom's shoulders. "I'm just so nervous…"

I stifle a sigh. At least if I give in, it won't be to Jasper. At least not today. "Listen, I'll stay. Or better yet, let's all go out. My treat."

It's the least I can do.

CHAPTER TEN

Jasper

THE FLASHES FROM THE CAMERAS ARE BLINDING, WHICH makes me wish I'd brought sunglasses. It's totally absurd to wish for sunglasses at ten o'clock in the evening, but the photographers outside my friend Sebastian's brand-new restaurant in Midtown are relentless.

Dominic nudges me with my elbow. "Don't look so pained. People will wonder if it's about the food."

"I haven't even gone in yet."

"They don't care about that."

Nothing affects Dominic Wilder—not the photographers, not anything. Well, except his wife, Vivienne, who looks every inch a fashion model as the two of them pose for the cameras. There's another barrage of clicks, and then Vivienne steers Dominic toward the entrance of the restaurant, catching my elbow with her other arm. "Come on. I'm starving."

He laughs, looking down at her with light in his eyes that sends a spike of envy straight through my gut. "You just ate."

"Three hours ago...and what's it to you, anyway?" Their good-natured teasing just reminds me of Isabella. Although, I wouldn't call what happened in my office good-natured. Or teasing. Unless you also call a rainstorm a hurricane.

Dominic and Vivienne's voices wash over me, blending with the crowd as we move through the restaurant to the cordoned-off section in the back reserved for friends of Sebastian's and investors. I count as both.

We've got a table for three, right on the other side of the velvet rope, and Dominic and I face each other with Vivienne between us. There's one empty seat because I didn't bring a date. Like an idiot, I didn't bring a date, which is making Dominic wonder if something is up.

"Stop looking at me like that."

"Like what?"

I exaggerate his narrow-eyed, assessing gaze. "Do you think I'm going to run off with the silverware?"

"Something's on your mind, clearly."

"Business."

Vivienne wags a finger in my direction. "False. You've had all day to think about business. Something else is eating you alive, Jasper."

"Don't you get started. I don't need the FBI involved in this."

She cracks a pretty smile, leaning back to let the waiter pour us what turns out to be a complimentary round of champagne from Sebastian. "Aha. So there *is* something to be involved in."

"At least don't start on him until we've had something to eat." Dominic picks up the printed menu in front of him. It's a four-course beauty meant to show off Sebastian's skill in the kitchen, and my mouth waters just from scanning my eyes over the text.

What would Isabella be interested in? The thought comes to me so automatically, so naturally, that I don't realize I'm thinking about her until several seconds later, when it's too late to stave off a raging erection. I pull my seat closer to the table and will myself to stop—stop thinking of her smooth voice, stop thinking of the way she'd look perched on all fours on my bed, the way she'd be a wild animal behind closed doors. No. I *cannot* spend the entire meal thinking about those things, or else—

The salad course comes out a moment later, and I shove the menu away. "That was fast."

The waiter grins down at me. "Sebastian left a note." He probably also mentioned that this table would have plenty when it came time to tip.

My cock pulses in my pants. "I'll be right back."

Dominic has been murmuring something into Vivienne's ear, but he breaks off and gives me a nod. "You all right?"

"Yeah. I'll be back in a minute."

This is not going to be one of my most shining moments. Not

by far. But I'm not going to be able to eat a damn thing unless I do something to take the pressure off.

There's a gaggle of women outside the narrow hallway to the restrooms—which, as far as I know, are private—and none of them see me coming.

"Excuse me."

Five pairs of eyes turn toward me, and as they back off, murmuring a chorus of apologies, I can see that any one of them might be willing to...

Irrelevant. Because none of them are Isabella Gabriel.

I cut through the center of their gathering and head for the men's room. I'm halfway down the hall when the door to the women's room opens with a violent swish and someone barrels out of it, straight into me. I catch her by the elbow on instinct, taking her weight in my grip.

"Excuse me—"

That's all she has time to say before her eyes meet mine and the rest of the world falls away.

I'll be damned.

"Isabella." I straighten up immediately and give her a wide grin, like I haven't just been rushing to the bathroom to jack off thinking of her.

One corner of her mouth rises in a surprised smile, and she pulls her clutch purse to her side. "Jasper Pace. What are you doing here?"

"Outside the women's bathroom? I was minding my own business, and—"

"At Sebastian's opening."

"Oh. I invested in the restaurant. He's a friend of a friend. We both came out to show our support."

Her eyes narrow. "A friend of a friend?"

"What are you, the restaurant opening police?"

She laughs. "Hardly. I'm just trying to figure out how we could possibly have ended up at the same function. It's so random." There's a barb in her voice, but all it does is make me want to press her up against the wall right now, the hell with the audience.

I shrug one shoulder. "Maybe Sebastian knows someone who needs a seamstress."

Her mouth drops open half an inch, and I want to put my thumb between her teeth, let her bite down.

"Pardon me." The low voice behind me leaves only one choice, and it's the perfect one. I step closer to Isabella, half a step between us at most, and let him squeeze by.

She's inches away, and even after he's gone, I don't step back. Her eyes are on mine, and there's a pink blush to her cheeks that tells me I'm not the only one who's been thinking.

"Do you have enough room?" She cuts her eyes down to the front of my pants. I'm hard as a rock, and it's obvious.

"I have too much room." I turn slightly away, adjusting myself, and then I lean in. "What would you think about a change in terms?" I could take her into that bathroom right now and lock the door. Her nipples are hard beneath the fabric of her dress, and her breaths are coming shallow and quick. "We could start the clock on that month right now."

It's a risk, and I know it. It shows too much of my hand. But I need her.

Isabella's eyes go wide.

CHAPTER ELEVEN

Isabella

J ASPER IS TOO CLOSE, AND AT THIS RANGE EVERYTHING ABOUT him is making me breathless.

I can't stand it.

I can't stand it, and I want more of it at the same time.

I can't believe he's going to be the first one to cede the higher ground like this, and at a restaurant opening, of all places.

I can't believe I'm about to say yes. The word is on the tip of my tongue, because my entire body is humming with the scent of him, the sight of him, his muscles lithe and strong beneath the outrageously expensive fabric of his suit. I'd like to take his lapels in my fists and swing him right into the women's restroom and straddle him on the first available surface.

I stop myself from speaking just in time to get the slightest grip on the situation. My panties, beneath the red halter dress I'm wearing just for this occasion, are soaked. And it's far too early in whatever twisted game we're playing to give in and fuck him.

No matter how badly I want to. The need curls in the pit of my gut, but I bite back the *yes* and straighten up against the wall. I don't have any more room to move backward, to create any space between us, but at least lifting my chin might give the illusion...

I cock my head to the side. "Changing the terms? Mr. Pace, I didn't think you were that kind of man."

"The kind of man who doesn't wait to take what he wants?"

"The kind of man who can't even make it through a week without renegotiating."

His eyes, sharp and shining in the dim light of the hallway, narrow, and he leans in. "Look me in the eye and tell me you're not wet right now, imagining what we could do behind a locked door."

"I'm not wet, imagining that." It's a half-truth, because I'm wetter with every word out of his mouth. It's far beyond wetness at this point. It's not like I saw a sexy man on the subway and let myself get a little carried away. It's like that man is in my bedroom with me, his fingers between my legs, playing me like a violin.

Jasper sets his jaw, gaze burning into mine for one more long moment, and then he stands up to his full height, stepping back into the hallway.

I catch my breath.

I try not to make it obvious.

I'm sure he's going to turn and go back to his dinner without another word.

Once again, he proves me wrong by extending his arm to me. "Join us."

I let out a laugh that's almost too loud for the size of the hallway. "First, who is *us*? And second, what makes you think I'm here alone?"

The smile that plays across his lips sends another jolt through me. "I'm here with Dominic Wilder and his wife, Vivienne. You might have heard of them." He hasn't pulled his arm back. "And I know you're here alone because you've got your purse in a tight little fist, like leaving it at your table was too much of a risk."

I give him a look. "I could have my purse with me for any number of reasons."

"Not a purse that size."

He's right. "I'm not alone."

"But you're here with strangers...or at least acquaintances. And my guess is that they won't lose too much sleep over it if you switch tables in the middle of a restaurant opening."

Right again. I'm seated at a table for six, and every other person is either with a date or came as part of the businesswomen's association I'm a part of. "It would be unspeakably rude to just disappear." Then I reach out and take his arm anyway. "We can stop by on the way back to your table."

Jasper leads me back out into the restaurant, and I tug him

in the opposite direction, away from the cordoned-off area for all the fanciest friends of Sebastian. My table is snugged up against the opposite wall. I lean down to one of the women I was chatting with before. If it wasn't for the *Jennifer* scrawled on her name tag, I wouldn't remember the first thing about her. "I'm moving tables—I just wanted to let you know."

She smiles up at me. "Oh, it was so nice meeting you. I hope—" Her eyes go wide when she catches sight of Jasper. "Wow. I—"

I pull my hand away from his arm and pull a business card out of my clutch purse. "Stay in touch, Jennifer."

Jasper tucks my arm back into his elbow and steers me away from the table. As we step behind the velvet ropes, it's like the room volume drops—even though that should be impossible. He leans in. "Ready to meet my friends?"

I grin at him like it's the most exciting thing he's ever asked me to do. "Don't be surprised if they're my friends more than yours by the end of this."

* * *

By the end of it, on the cab ride home, I'm burning up.

I chatted with Dominic and Vivienne, warming up to Dominic's dark-haired and whip-smart wife in the first two minutes. No surprise that she works for the FBI. I'm a little surprised that she and Dominic could sit and chat for so long. The way his eyes stayed on her, drinking in her every move—it's clear he's obsessed with her.

I just hope they didn't notice that it took a Herculean effort to keep my hands off Jasper. I didn't want to let go of his arm when we sat down at the table. I wanted to keep my hand right there until it was time to get in a cab and go...wherever he wanted.

Not a chance of that.

I squirm against the seat of my own cab, waiting to finally move through the last two torturous blocks before my apartment. The moment the driver pulls up to the curb I'm out of the car, bill already paid with the credit card scanner in the back, and leaning in to shove a tip into his hand.

The elevator doors don't have time to close behind me before I'm inside my apartment, slamming the door shut and twisting the lock on the deadbolt. My purse tumbles to the floors.

I have a date that I can't put off any longer.

In my bedroom, I grab the vibrator from the top drawer of my dresser. I've been telling myself not to use it, not to get that deep into fantasies about Jasper, but I can't.

I could have been with him tonight.

I could have been having hot, raw sex in the bathroom at the restaurant, and who knows what else in his penthouse...or even my place. But I couldn't do it. I couldn't let the tension slack between us, couldn't give in. It's like I'm being torn in two.

I hike up my dress, laying back against the comforter of my bed, and spread my legs wide, shoving the vibrator between the lace of my panties and my skin. My mind is flooded with Jasper—Jasper's piercing blue eyes, the animal strength of him beneath his suits, the way I know he'd take me, command me, if I could just give in...

It should be him, not a vibrator, but I ride it to a burst of pleasure, a hint of release, and curl up on the bed, breathing hard.

Three more days...

CHAPTER TWELVE

Jasper

TEN MINUTES, AND EVERYTHING STARTS.

Ten minutes, and this agonizing week is finally at an end.

As long as Isabella shows up.

From the red-hot glow on her face as we sat through dinner together at the restaurant opening that lasted a hundred years, she's just as interested in this as I am—although I don't ever expect her to admit it. Still, this game—this push and pull that keeps me up at night—could end right now, if she chose.

All she has to do is stay home.

Or anywhere other than my penthouse, really.

Ten minutes before nine, and I'm forcing myself to stay seated in the living room, looking out over the Manhattan skyline. Spring is rushing into summer, and I'm barreling toward *something* with Isabella. I'm just not sure if it's a train crash or a smooth takeoff.

I laugh a little, even though there's nobody in the room to hear it. Smooth is not the way we operate. With Isabella, every interaction is a battle that's tinged with a desire so hot that sometimes I think it might melt my clothes off.

Which would be fine, as long as it melted hers off, too.

I kept contact to a minimum after the opening on Tuesday, texting her only once—nine o'clock, with the address to my penthouse. I didn't give any instructions on what to wear. I want to see what she'll choose for myself.

Another glance at my watch. Two minutes have gone by. Eight to go.

If I know anything about Isabella—and granted, what I do know about her is limited to a handful of charged interactions and a Google search that basically revealed that yes, she is a successful businesswoman in New York City—then she won't be a minute early or a minute late.

Five minutes to go.

Even that assumption could be a toss-up. I know damn well that she must be doing everything she possibly can to keep me off balance. I know it because as much as I want to possess her, I can't help playing her game.

So maybe she won't be here on time. Maybe she'll be late.

I put my hands over my face and take a deep breath in. I'm Jasper Pace. No woman should have me this rattled. I exhale slowly, absolutely in control of the air exiting my lungs. No. I won't let it happen. A little infatuation, sure. A business deal that will get both of us what we want, even if the terms are a little unconventional—absolutely. Letting her run my mind like this? Not a chance. Not for another moment.

Three minutes to go.

I threw myself into work for the rest of the week to the point that Mike Ford, of all people, started to get a little testy when meetings ran over for the third day in a row. At the end of Thursday's meeting he slapped his folder shut on the desk and stayed seated until the rest of the team filed out of the meeting room. Mike's been with Pace, Inc. since I started, and he rarely puts up a fuss about anything.

He leveled his gaze at me. "What's this about, boss?"

The *boss* was meant to inject a little levity into the interaction, I think, but his dead-serious look overpowered it. I spread my hands wide. "I have goals, Mike. That's business as usual."

He narrowed his eyes. "Business as usual? I thought you wanted two more buildings by July, not five. It was five total just last week."

"You have a problem with picking up speed?"

"I have a problem with getting overextended." He tapped his fingers against the folder in front of him. "Look, I'm seeking out the best possible properties for you. You know I am. I haven't given you a reason to question my work—unless there's something you want to tell me."

I shook my head. "Flawless, as usual."

"I don't have to tell you that too much, too fast is a recipe for disaster."

"You think even these preliminary plans are too much?"

He leaned in, folding his hands on the table. "I think there's something else behind this. You're ruthless as hell, Jasper. Nobody's disputing that. I just don't want to see these renovations get out of control and cause..." He pressed his lips together into a firm line. "There's always a chance things turn out fine. But with everything we rush, we open ourselves up to a PR disaster or a building that comes in way over cost...or we miss opportunities. I want to do this right."

Anyone but Mike, and I'd have taken it personally. My father never fired anyone for disagreeing with him, either, which is just good business—but I knew Mike was sincere. "All valid points." The truth, anyway, was that I'd been pushing so hard to find new buildings to keep my mind off Isabella. Fat chance.

My phone buzzes with a request from the private elevator. It's one minute to nine.

My heart leaps into my throat.

I confirm the request from my phone and head for the entryway.

The doors slide open.

It's her.

Isabella is a fucking goddess in black. Her dress is simple—a sheath that hits just above her knees—but the way it hugs her curves is anything but. Her dark hair is swept back into a bun on the top of her head, not a wisp out of place. My hands ache with the urge to take it down, to let it fall over her shoulders, to tug it through my fingers until her head is tipped back, her red lips parted, breath shallow while she waits to discover what I'm going to do next. She has a purse over her shoulder, and low heels on. That's it. The weather has been very warm for May, even for the city, and she must not have needed a jacket, judging by the pink in her cheeks.

Her green eyes are alive with anticipation, and there's a little smile on her lips. But I see her hand trembling around the handle of her purse, just enough to notice.

"Am I on time?" Her low voice sends fingertips of heat over my spine.

I make a show of checking my watch as I move toward her, closing the distance between us, breathing more of her in with every step I take. "Right on time." I stop half a step away from her. She bites her lip, looking up at me, unflinching. "Are you ready to begin?"

Isabella nods, just once.

"I'll take your purse." She extends it toward me, and I take it, setting it aside on the small table against the wall. Then I'm looking into her eyes again. "One last chance." The suggestion is soft, gentle.

"I'm ready."

"Good. Then get down on your knees."

CHAPTER THIRTEEN

Isabella

MY HEART THUDS AGAINST MY RIB CAGE, DROWNING OUT everything except Jasper's words, echoing again and again in my head. *Get down on your knees. Get down on your knees. Get down on your knees.*

This is what I've been fantasizing about since last Friday, even if I'll never, ever admit it to anyone. And now that the moment has arrived, it's like I've discovered at the last minute that instead of jumping off the side of the pool, I'm going to be skydiving. I don't even have the safety of my purse to hold anymore.

My muscles are tensed, and I suck in a breath, trying to steady myself. If this is what it's going to take to save my mother's home, then I shouldn't waste any more time. I should just do it. And deep down, in the darkest part of my mind, I want this. I've wanted it since the moment the energy between Jasper and me crackled through the air in his office and struck me like a bolt of lightning. Another thing I'll never admit out loud.

All I have to do is get down on my knees. I can feel how plush the carpeting is even through my heels. It's not going to hurt anything, except maybe the last remnants of pride I'm still clinging to. And why? The idea of this has kept me wet and hot and bothered for a week.

I guess it's different when it's actually happening.

I look into Jasper's eyes for another heartbeat. His jaw, which may as well be chiseled straight out of a flawless piece of marble, is set in a commanding line. I get the impression that he could wait all day for me to obey him.

He might expect me to linger over this, to hesitate, to balk at the last second.

No. I can't have that.

I lower my eyes to the carpet and sink to my knees in front of him, my heart pulsing even louder, rolling thunder in my head. The carpet gives under my bare legs. It's more luxurious than some of the nicer beds I've slept on since Gabriel Luxe took off.

"Good." The single word from his lips sends satisfaction spreading through my chest, and I don't even know why. I haven't needed anyone's praise in a long time. It looks like we're through the looking glass. "You look gorgeous, on your knees like that."

I open my mouth, but I'm not sure what to say. I don't know the rules of a game like this, so I'm going to have to let Jasper lead the way. I have the sense that I should keep my gaze lowered, so I do, right up until—

"Look at me," he commands. I tip my head back, meeting Jasper's eyes. An arresting blue, burning with lust, and a strange smile quirks the corner of his mouth. *He thinks he's won.* Well, he hasn't won. I might want his hands on my body, but I haven't forgotten the end goal—to take him for all he's worth, and my mother's building besides. No matter how molten hot my core is right now, I can't ever forget that. And I never will.

Behind the blazing need lighting up his eyes is something darker, something without limits, without boundaries, but it doesn't scare me. In fact, it makes me straighten my back. I have no idea what's going to happen next. I have no idea if Jasper has some kind of sex dungeon in his penthouse, or if he's going to take me right here in the entryway and send me back out. Things could get really kinky. The pulse in my throat gets stronger. *Am I going to stroke out just from the anticipation?* Wouldn't that be a pretty way to burn this deal to the ground. My body trembles in my struggle to keep from leaping to my feet and throwing my arms around his neck. I don't know whether I want to kiss him or slap him for making me feel this way, making me feel so torn.

"You're mine now," he says it casually, like he's reminding me to take an umbrella in case it rains.

"Yes." I can't look away from him, and I can't say nothing—it's not as if he's commanded me to stay silent, or anything. Now the grin on his face turns wicked before it flickers back into a serious expression.

"There's so much we could do."

I swallow hard, another cascade of images tumbling through my mind, another burst of wetness between my legs. "Yes." He's got to be testing me, to see what will make me snap, make me laugh, make me say no. I don't do any of those things. Yet.

"And here you are, kneeling in my entryway in your pretty dress, looking up at me with color in your cheeks...does this turn you on, Isabella?"

Not that we've gone over every detail, but part of this has to be honesty. It has to be, otherwise the entire thing is going to crumble under the weight of wildly mismatched expectations. I haven't been in the habit of lying to Jasper—or anyone else—no matter how we might be dancing around each other, pushing each other's buttons. So I go with the truth, the only embellishment a little more shame in my tone than I actually feel. "Yes."

That smile, that wide, smoldering smile, spreads across his face. "Good. That's exactly how I want you to feel when you're with me." He steps closer, and I can't catch my breath. It's going to start, and it's going to start right now. I press my hands against my thighs. *What is he going to tell me to do next?* I have a feeling that no matter what it is, I'll just do it. Hesitating is making me so wound up I'm cutting off the air supply to my own brain.

Jasper reaches down and strokes my cheek with the back of his knuckles, his touch feather-light but leaving a trail of burning skin behind it. He traces all the way around to the back of my head, where my neck is bare, and draws one finger down my spine toward the neckline of my dress. Goosebumps rise along the skin there, trailing all the way down to the base of my spine.

He toys with the zipper.

Holy shit. My cheeks are so hot they have to be beet red. *Is he going to strip me down right here in the entryway?* It's not as if I didn't wear a lacy bra and matching panties, bought just today at a boutique down the block from my headquarters. I'd just expected...I don't know, a bedroom.

Then he steps to my side, and the next thing I register is his hand extended down toward me, palm up. "Come with me."

I put my hand in his and get carefully to my feet, trying to ignore the little wobble in my knees.

Jasper steps forward, into the penthouse and I take a deep breath.

Don't hesitate. Not even a little.

CHAPTER FOURTEEN

Jasper

I SABELLA'S HAND IS SHAKING IN MINE, AND THE SENSATION HAS me harder than steel. My own anticipation is getting difficult to contain, but at least we're in my territory. For the first time since we met, I'm calling all the shots.

It's a welcome opportunity, at least for the moment, to keep her on her toes.

We step into the living area. "Wow." The word is a whisper, her eyebrows raised. "That's an incredible view."

I shrug playfully. "It's not bad. I prefer the view out of my villa in France." *Villa* hardly does justice to the property, which I only get to a few times a year, but it's true—the Mediterranean sparkling below a summer sunrise beats Manhattan any day.

Isabella rolls her eyes, a flick of her gaze toward the ceiling.

"I would have given anything to even visit a place like this when I was growing up."

It's such a genuine statement, not a hint of a double meaning, that I take a second to look at her. She's still looking toward the windows, the last of the sunset reflected in her face. Isabella catches me watching. Her green eyes go serious again. It was probably a way for her to buy some time, let her racing heart slow a little bit. The pulse fluttering in her neckline isn't quite so hard now.

At least it wasn't until she looked at me.

Isabella Gabriel might be the most audacious woman ever to shove past my secretary and demand a meeting with me—if I'm honest, she's the only woman who's ever done that—but this cannot possibly be what she thought she was getting into. Hell, I'm not sure *I* even realized what we'd be getting into. It's a sheer delight watching her cheeks heat up.

"Well, now your dream has come true."

Isabella laughs, but there's an element of her nervousness there that she can't hide.

"Moving along." She hasn't pulled her hand away from mine, so it's a simple matter of tugging her in the direction we're going—through the sunken living room, to the left, and up another two steps into the hallway there. Isabella takes a big breath in and lets it out slowly as we move down the hallway. Energy is radiating off of her, heating up the corridor, and it's like she's dying to ask me where this leads.

The hallway opens into...

...my dining room.

Isabella hesitates for the first time as we cross the threshold. She does more than hesitate, in fact. She stops dead, two steps in, her eyes flicking suspiciously across the space.

Because the dining room isn't exactly empty.

My massive dining table, which can seat twelve, has been replaced with a smaller one just in front of a window boasting another spectacular view of the Manhattan skyline. The rest of the space has been converted into a kind of sitting area, a sofa and a wingback chair arranged around a glass-top coffee table reflecting the light of the gas fireplace, turned on low.

If she was expecting the master bedroom, or some kind of playroom, this is not it.

The final touch is the uniformed waiter bending over the table, pouring white wine into our respective glasses.

Isabella presses her lips together like she's trying not to smile, but her eyes are narrowed as she takes it all in with another sweep of her gaze. It's all I can do not to keep from laughing. The arrangement we made was not for a private meal, although I never said it wouldn't include one. This has to be the final straw, the thing that pushes her into full-blown confusion. There's no way she was expecting this.

She takes her bottom lip between her teeth, then steps closer to me. *What is this?* I'd bet a thousand dollars that those will be the next words out of her mouth.

"So," she says, her tone soft and sensual, like she's still kneeling on the carpet in the entryway, looking up at me from the floor. "Where do you want me? On the table, or on the sofa? Oh—or the chair?"

Damn. Is she completely unshakeable?

"Seated. At the table, not on it." I lean in so that I'm murmuring right into her ear. "You can keep your clothes on...for now."

That puts a little more blush in her cheeks, but she lets me escort her over to the table without another word. "Mr. Pace." The waiter, Conrad, straightens as we approach. "Ms. Gabriel. Are you ready for the first course?"

The first course is my personal chef Lucas's favorite salad—something involving candied pears—and I can't wait to watch Isabella eat them, the shining fruit against her perfect lips. "Yes," I tell him. "Bring it out." He moves smoothly away while I pull Isabella's chair out from under the table so she can sit. I've just taken my seat when Conrad comes back, the small plates balanced in his hands.

Isabella looks over the delicate arrangement. "Impressive."

"Not as impressive as you," I say, not missing a beat.

She smiles at me across the table. "I haven't done anything impressive yet."

"I disagree. You barged into my office without an appointment."

Her shoulders relax a little, and a fraction of the tension goes out of the air. "So this is a date?"

"What makes you think that?"

"Oh…office talk. A dinner in your private dining room. It doesn't seem like—" She breaks off, as if searching for just the right word.

"The kind of arrangement where I possess you for an entire month?"

She picks up her fork, looking up at me with fire in her eyes. "No. It doesn't seem like that." I'm guessing this is as close as she'll get to admitting her surprise.

"An arrangement like that can't include dinner?" I grin at her, picking up my own fork and spearing a section of candied pear. "My goodness, Isabella. We hardly know each other. Shouldn't we get that out of the way first?"

Isabella cocks her head to the side. "I'm not the kind of woman you can get to know over the course of one meal."

"We'll see about that."

She laughs. "What about you, Jasper Pace? Are you the kind of man who can be summarized in a single dinner?"

"Depends on what you want to know."

"I want to know what makes you so relentless. I checked up on you during our…time apart. You're terrorizing all of New York City with your insistence on gutting all the best buildings."

"If by *best* you mean *in most need of improvement.*"

"Whatever lets you sleep at night."

"What's your lullaby, Isabella? Is it the sound of all the cash you're raking in from Gabriel Luxe?"

She narrows her eyes with a smile. "You did your research, too."

"Of course I did. What I couldn't find was why."

"Why what?"

"Why are *you* so hell-bent on expansion? How did you get into fashion, anyway?"

Isabella purses her lips. "I'm not just into fashion. I'm into... fitness. And business. And utility. I think clothes should be simpler, and higher quality."

"Was that always a passion of yours?"

"No. Paying the bills was." She slips a section of candied pear between her lips and swallows. "That's damn good. Anyway, my mother had practically no money when I was growing up. I had to do something."

"And that something was fashion?"

She shrugs. "She had a sewing machine."

It's a good thing she didn't have a collection of tanks, because Isabella Gabriel would have taken over the world.

"Okay. I'll admit it. I was wrong," I say.

Isabella laughs. "About what?"

"This is going to take more than one dinner."

CHAPTER FIFTEEN

Isabella

I DON'T UNDERSTAND THE FIRST THING ABOUT JASPER, THAT much is clear.

We move through the salad course and he asks me more about what it was like growing up. "*Very* luxe." I give him a sage glance, and he laughs. "We had a one-bedroom in the Bronx, and we all shared the bedroom."

"We all…"

"My sister Evie, my mom, and me."

"You have a sister? Any brothers?"

"Yes, and no. Just the two of us. My dad didn't stick around long enough for me to remember anything about him."

"Wow."

"Very courageous. A real man's man." More bitterness than I'd intended creeps into my tone, and I'm not sure why. "Your father seems pretty...involved."

"I can't complain about him. Sometimes I wonder what he's looking for."

"In terms of..."

A flash of frustration crosses Jasper's face. "I don't know what I'm saying. Everything is Pace, Inc. for him."

"Just like it is for you?"

His blue eyes dance. "I'm here with you—doesn't that tell you anything?"

"It tells me you're honoring the terms of the deal."

Jasper leans back for the waiter—whose name I learned is Conrad—to slide small bowls of what turns out to be the best butternut squash soup I've ever had. "My father would never have made a deal that took up this much of his evening."

So that's where he gets some of his relentless attitude from. It's just the way it's always been.

"What about your mother?"

Jasper's face darkens, just for a moment. "What about her?"

I have to tread carefully here, clearly. "Do you see her often?" I'm half-expecting him to say that she's dead.

"Almost never."

A heavy silence lingers between us then, and I lift another spoonful of butternut squash soup to my lips. It's so damn delicious that I almost forget I've tripped some unseen wire in the conversation.

Right up until Jasper continues.

"She spends most of her time traveling in Europe."

"And the rest of it?"

"God knows."

I take a sip of wine. "We don't have to talk about this if—"

Jasper waves me off. "It's not a big deal. She had an affair when I was thirteen and my parents divorced shortly after. My dad didn't even deny her alimony, which she took every two weeks until she remarried when I was in college. That guy's dead now—heart attack—but she never gave up her traveling lifestyle."

"My mother just retired last summer."

A flicker of relief crosses his face. "What did she do?"

"She taught elementary school."

Jasper makes a face. "I can't imagine."

"I can't either. But it's what she wanted to do. Half the reason we had no money for stretches of time growing up was because she went back to school to get a better job."

"And while she was in school, you were—what, hunched over a sewing machine in some closet somewhere, making a fortune?"

I laugh. "It wasn't a fortune at first, and I didn't work in a closet. I worked in our front hallway."

"Making..."

"Clothes." He gives me a look. "I bought remnants from the fabric shops and made these clothes for the women who exercised in the neighborhood. They used to walk around the block, or around the park. If one of them had a baby they'd take the stroller, too. But they wanted to look cool while they did it, and nobody was making clothes like that at the time, with different patterns and colors. Everything I made was, obviously, a unique piece."

"None of your lines now have wild colors."

I grin at him, and he looks down at his soup. "You caught me. I browsed your website."

"You had no choice. What if you were entering some kind of weird sex treaty with some kind of fashion serial killer? That has to come through in their designs."

Jasper's gaze is piercing. "It's hardly a weird sex treaty."

"Isn't it?"

"We haven't had sex yet," he reminds me. I pretend to be absorbed in another spoonful of soup, but the turn this conversation has taken has me off-balance again, slick between my legs and slightly lightheaded. Sex with Jasper is guaranteed to be mind-blowing. Just the way he moves in his clothes, the way his grasp is powerful even when he's just holding my hand, makes me certain of it.

"Yet." My voice is too soft, and I clear my throat. We're in Jasper's penthouse, in his dining room, which is empty except for the two of us and occasionally Conrad. *Yet* could end at any moment, and my entire body is buzzing with the possibility. Images flash one by one into my mind: my own knuckles white on the edge of the table. My bare knees against the hardwood floor. The smooth leather of the wingback chair meeting my bare skin. We might be in the middle of dinner right now, but that doesn't mean…

Conrad swoops in, clearing the empty bowls of soup and re-placing them with the main course: steak so tender and perfect that it has to have cost a fortune. Every bite is a little taste of paradise.

Jasper goes back to asking me first-date questions, but that doesn't make my heart beat any slower.

"Have you been dating for long?"

I laugh out loud, my fork clanging against the edge of my plate. "This is not dating."

His eyes sparkle. "I don't think you'd have entered into this with me if you were engaged, or seeing someone seriously." He cocks his head to the side, considering me for a long moment. "Maybe I'm wrong. Maybe you would."

"I wouldn't." The memory of Jason's idiotic face swims up in my memory.

"Whoa. Is the steak not up to par?"

"No, that's not—the steak is probably the best thing I've ever eaten in my life. You reminded me of—of the last relationship I was in."

"I take it things didn't end well."

"You could say that."

By the time our plates are empty and Conrad is carrying them quickly back to...well, the kitchen, I assume, my heart is back to hammering against my rib cage. And when Jasper stands up and offers me his hand, I have to take a big breath before I can bring myself to stand up.

"There *was* something I was going to suggest," I say to break the silence while we walk back out toward the living room. *Where is his bedroom from here?* "I think you should come with me to another function I'm invited to. It's tomorrow night."

Jasper's eyes go wide. "A public function?"

"Well, yes."

I'm so busy waiting for his reply that it takes me a moment to realize he's taken me right back to the front door, that he's handing me my purse, that he's leaning in to kiss me on the forehead.

When he steps back, I know I'm giving him a bewildered look. "I'm leaving?"

"Dinner was wonderful, wasn't it?"

"Yes, but—" I snap my mouth closed. "Yes."

He presses the button for the elevator, and the doors slide open. "I'll check my schedule for tomorrow."

Then they're sliding shut again, me on the other side, and Jasper's face disappears from view.

CHAPTER SIXTEEN

Jasper

ANOTHER BANK OF CAMERAS, EVEN MORE OF THEM FLASHING in my face. Many more than were at Sebastian's opening last week.

"You are *such* a liar," I murmur into Isabella's ear, a wide grin on my face. I know exactly how it's going to play on the gossip sites when the photos hit later tonight—*Billionaire Jasper Pace flirts publicly with new lover.*

"I didn't lie about anything." She keeps her smile on, too, leaning in a little closer so that each of them gets a few shots of her practically nuzzling my neck. *Isabella Gabriel's new beau is a billionaire with ties to real estate...*

We move a few more steps down the red carpet, which I personally think is a little much for an industry awards ceremony, but I'm not going to say that out loud. Not here. "You said this was a small event."

"I said it was a smaller industry event."

"As opposed to—"

"I don't know, Paris Fashion Week?"

We both laugh together, her face illuminated in the camera flashes, and my heart turns over in my chest.

It killed me to send her on her way at the end of dinner. Killed me. I could have died from the sheer lust I'd been containing all through dinner only to end up blueballed and alone at the end. It was according to plan, but that doesn't mean I liked it. At all.

I also wasn't partial to the flash of understanding that moved across her eyes like a thunderstorm in miniature as the elevator doors closed. If she thinks she understood, then...

I don't know. Maybe she did. That's the infuriating and intoxicating thing about Isabella. I'm never sure where exactly we stand in this game, and I love it and hate it simultaneously.

According to plan, yes, but I didn't make that decision until toward the end of the meal, when every cell in my body was screaming at me to take her back to my bedroom and fuck her until she was ruined for all other men. But something stopped me cold. It was the overwhelming sense that if I did that, we'd have crossed a line too early in the game, and it might send us rushing toward a premature end.

Not that I think Isabella is going to back out. But I couldn't ignore the feeling. I couldn't ignore it, so I sent her home. A move neither of us could possibly have expected.

I still don't know why I care if she backs out early. I never thought she'd accept in the first place. Now we're here, out in public, on a date that's a thousand times more real than a behind-the-scenes dinner in my apartment, and I don't hate it. I don't hate the camera flashes. I don't hate the fact that we're going to be the subjects of all the gossip outlets in the city by morning, if not by midnight.

I can't explain it. I wouldn't even begin to explain it to someone like my father. He'd probably just remind me that nothing matters except business.

We step off the carpet and into the lobby of the Lincoln Center, where Isabella dives right in. I underestimated her when she first walked into my office. I might not know much about the fashion industry, but I know quite a few big-name designers and fashion house owners. Some of them are here, and all of them recognize Isabella Gabriel. She kisses cheek after cheek, holding hands with elegant woman after elegant woman in gown after eye-catching gown. They're all wishing her good luck.

When I finally offer her my arm again, she's glowing. "And you still think you're not a liar?"

Isabella looks up at me with wide, innocent eyes. "About *what*?"

"You made me think you were just some down-on-her-luck fashion designer."

"What did I ever do to give you that impression?"

All of my memories of her collide into a swirling slideshow, her voice overlaying the entire thing. It hits me like a tidal wave. She never said she was down on her luck. Maybe the timing with that building in Hamilton Heights wasn't the best for her, but she's clearly not a woman trying desperately to climb the rungs. She's got a place in the world, and it's a damn good one.

So why did she feel like she needed to say yes to me?

I don't have time to think about it, because there's a movement to the hall where the ceremony and dinner are taking place. Isabella makes conversation with just about every person around us on the way there, and the constant flow of conversation continues all through dinner.

It should be boring as hell, but watching Isabella is a sight to behold. I can imagine her at fifteen, charming everyone in the Bronx to help pay the rent and groceries. I've done well for myself at Pace, Inc., but I never had to reach as far as she did. She's radiant. She's in her element. She's my date.

Technically, I guess, I'm *her* date.

Suddenly, while I'm in the midst of thinking about how I'd love to steal her away to some dark alcove and push the understated pink gown she's wearing up to her waist, she's standing up from her seat, all the lights in the house on her. Everyone around the table is clapping. I join in only a second too late. The woman seated on my other side—Clarisse?—clutches my arm. "Can you believe it?"

"I can." I answer even though I have no idea what Isabella has just won, other than that it seems like a big deal. She's presented with a crystal trophy up on the stage, and her award is announced again—Best Designer Under 30 for the entire year. Damn.

She steps up to the podium, absolutely beaming. "Thank you so much." That's all I hear, because I'm lost in the sight of her in the spotlight, her back straight, her hair and makeup flawless, everything about her projecting confidence and drive. I can't be the only one in the room wondering which award she'll take home next year—if she's even still in the city. She could be anywhere across the planet, selling anything.

That's all I hear until she takes a deep breath and looks out into the crowd. "And finally, I'd like to thank Jasper Pace." All around me, heads swivel in my direction. "For giving me a brand-new fire." She smiles for another long moment. "Thank you."

Applause erupts all around me, and my cock jumps in my pants.

I have to get my hands on her.

Or at least the surprise I have hidden in my pocket.

CHAPTER SEVENTEEN

Isabella

J ASPER'S EYES ARE FLASHING WHEN I GET BACK TO THE TABLE.
For a sickening instant, my stomach drops into my toes. Is he
that pissed?

But when I slide into my seat, all it takes is one glance at the
front of his pants to see that he's not angry with me. He's just as
turned on as I am, just as ready to get the hell out of here and
go somewhere without any prying eyes. In my case, it's not so
obvious.

Jasper leans in, and I breathe in the clean, pure scent of his
skin. It was torture, out there on the red carpet, to get so close to
him without pressing my lips to the side of his neck, or wrapping
my hands around his face and pulling him in for a kiss. The kind
of kiss you don't do in front of photographers unless you really,
really mean it. "Tell me this ceremony is almost over."

"It's almost over," I say.

"Tell me the truth."

"There are ten more awards. Haven't you been following along in the program?"

"No. I've been looking at you," he says, his voice laced with a husky warmth.

"All this time? I look exactly the same as when we walked in."

"No, you don't. You've got a very fancy crystal trophy for being such a successful fashion designer." I laugh. "I can't believe you didn't tell me about all this," he adds.

"What was I supposed to say? You never know whether you're going to win in advance."

"You had some kind of idea."

"Well, I didn't decide to expand across the state for no reason. My designs are really quite popular. But what sets me apart from a lot of these people is that I'm managing all the aspects of production and distribution by myself."

He shakes his head. "What other secrets are you hiding, Isabella?"

"I should ask you the same question." There's got to be something underneath all this, something that drives him to be the way he is.

"I'm an open book."

I laugh out loud, but the sound is covered by another round of applause for someone who's just won the next award. "Jasper Pace, an open book? No."

He drops his voice so I have to lean closer, my hand on his arm. "Here's how much of an open book I am." I breathe in, warmth already rising to my cheeks. "I don't want to wait for another ten—nine—awards. I want to take you outside right now and get into my town car."

"And then what?" I hear my voice laced with anticipation.

"Then I'll take you wherever you want to go."

I bite my lip. "You want to leave...right now?"

"Yes. As soon as humanly possible," he says, almost a growl.

"Me too," I say and he starts to stand, but I keep a gentle pressure on his arm and he stays in his seat. "The thing is, it won't look good if I bail on this after I've been presented with my own award." I sigh. "I do want to go. But I can't. We have to stay."

He grits his teeth and forces a smile. "That's not a problem. I just need you to come with me for a couple of minutes."

Fine. I'll bite. When he stands up, I put my hand in his and let him lead me away.

He clearly knows where he's going—and where he's going turns out to be a pitch-dark alcove down the hall from the main room. Jasper presses me up against the wall, my hands pressed back against it. He's so close. "What is this? Some kind of punishment?" I try to keep my voice steady, but it trembles, just a little.

"Hardly. Spread your legs."

It takes me a heartbeat to do it, but the energy arcing through me is so intense, so sexual, that the last thing on earth I'm going to do is disobey.

I brace myself against the wall and move my legs apart a foot. "Farther."

Another few inches, and I can feel the air moving up underneath my dress and between my legs.

Jasper reaches down and lifts the hem of my gown, sliding his hand up my leg until his fingers make contact with my panties. I can't stifle my gasp.

"Shh."

I press my lips together as he tugs my panties to the side, stroking along my now-exposed slit. I'm soaked. Jesus. My hands rise up to his shoulders so I can hold on for dear life. He leans down and presses his lips against my neck, gentle and hot.

"Yes. *Yes.*"

He works a finger inside of me, drawing it back out just as quickly. I'm surprised by the disappointment that tumbles through me when he moves away, but then his hand is back between my legs, pressing something inside. It feels smooth and cool, and when he takes his fingers back out it's firmly in place. He kisses me softly on the lips.

"What—"

"We should get back to your ceremony."

"Should we?" I move my hands away from his shoulders, taking his lapels in my fist, and throw my weight against him. He goes back against the opposite wall, making contact with a *thud*, and then I crush my mouth against his. Screw the soft, gentle kisses. I'm like an animal who's just been unleashed.

When I pull back, he's the one who's slightly out of breath.

"Okay," I say, hooking a finger into his lapel. "Now we can go."

I'm in mid-conversation with the woman next to me when I feel it—a buzz that radiates through my entire body, adding another layer to my already red cheeks. It takes me by surprise, making me forget what I'm saying in the middle of my sentence. I'm glad I'm not holding my wine glass. I'd have crushed it in my fist.

"Is something the matter?" the woman says, her eyebrows drawing together in concern.

"No. No, no." I laugh, waving a hand in the air. "What was I saying?"

The second time, it lasts even longer, and I turn to glare at Jasper. He holds my gaze until he turns it off, hand emerging from his pocket a moment later. "It's really a lovely ceremony." He says it with a wicked half-smile and sips his wine.

"It is."

There are still five more awards to go when he activates it for the third time, and I have to put my fingertips to my lips to stop any sound from escaping. Holy *shit*. I'm going to have a full-blown orgasm in the middle of an awards ceremony unless I can get out of here. *Now*.

When it turns off, I stand, murmuring apologies to the rest of the table. There's just enough time between the awards to escape from the hall, giving apologetic waves to everybody who makes eye contact with me. I know most of them. And I almost just came in front of all of them.

Jasper's town car is idling at the curb, and he holds the door open for me, letting me slide in and across before he climbs in and pulls the door shut behind him.

I can't stop myself.

"You have to be the most *sadistic*—"

"Terrence. Go." He doesn't say another word. He reaches out and pulls me closer, wrapping one arm around my waist and raising his other hand to stroke the side of my neck. I gasp, and an inferno of desire rushes through me when he wraps one hand around my jaw. He tilts my head back, against his shoulder, and then I feel him reaching for the switch in his pocket.

"Don't forget," he growls into my ear. "You're mine. Every inch of you, for the next twenty-eight days."

I can't speak. I can hardly breathe.

He turns my head toward him and leans down, kissing me so fiercely I almost come in his arms.

It can't get better than this.

CHAPTER EIGHTEEN

Jasper

M Y FINGERS ARE TOO HEAVY ON THE KEYBOARD, BUT I DON'T notice it until Mike is poking his head in the door to my office. When I glance up, he's looking at me with raised eyebrows. "Is something on your mind?" He tucks the stack of folders in his hand under his arm.

"No. Why?" This is a blatant lie, but the last thing Mike needs to know is that almost all of my focus is on Isabella. And Isabella's not even here.

I kissed her in the town car like I wanted to kiss her all damn night at that awards ceremony. I gave her one orgasm. I could have given her a hundred.

But I didn't take her back to my place. I'd given Terrence her address ahead of time, and that's where he knew to drive. I was so consumed by her that I didn't think to change the destination.

I shouldn't have changed it, anyway. It was the right thing to do to draw this out, to commit to the slow build.

That doesn't mean the decision hasn't been eating me alive.

Isabella texted me yesterday morning, just after eight. I normally don't get up early on Sundays, but I was already staring at the ceiling by then, the thought of my lips against hers making me hard under the comforter. It seemed sad as hell to get up just to get off without her, but I was heavily debating it. Until my phone vibrated on the bedside table.

Not on Sundays?

My heart leapt in my chest as the ball rocketed right back into my court. I could say that yes, she absolutely needed to be at my penthouse on Sundays—and every other day. There's just simply no way we could sustain that for a month, though, and if she was going to ask, there had to be some reason she wanted Sundays free. Something to do with her mother, I'd bet. So I told her no. No, not on Sundays.

Naturally, that meant I spent all day Sunday doing the same futile activities to try and forget her.

"You're typing like you're trying to press the keyboard right through your desk."

I save the email I'm typing and swivel away from the computer. "Mind your own business." I keep my tone light, and Mike grins, stepping into the office. "I take it you have that information."

"I do." He takes the seat across from me and puts the folders on the desk. "These are the summaries for the three properties you acquired in March."

"And the Hamilton Heights property was one of those."

"Yes." He flips open the top folder. "Two of them—the one in Hamilton Heights and the one in Spanish Harlem, were sold to Pace, Inc. by the same company—Brilliance NYC. Owned by a guy named Howard Knight."

I lean forward, crossing my arms on the surface of the desk. "And for both of these, he guaranteed us that the spaces were either unoccupied or that all leases would be finished by the first of May."

Mike opens another folder, scans one of the papers, and nods. "Hamilton Heights is totally unoccupied. The other property should be by now, since it's—" He glances down at my desk calendar. "—the second week of May."

"I seem to remember this guy saying this to me—did you set up a phone call with the two of us for some reason?"

"I think so. It was during the last stages of negotiation, and you wanted to confirm some of the details, as far as I recall."

"Okay. We might have a problem with these two buildings."

Mike's forehead wrinkles with concern. He was the one who found these two properties—among most of the others I've acquired in the past five years—and he does a damn good job. "What specifically? I vetted both of these for—"

"I know. I'm not sure how this...escaped our attention, but the Hamilton Heights building is still occupied."

His eyes go wide. "What?"

"Two weeks ago, the current owner sent out a lease termination notice. None of the residents are being allowed to renew. In August."

His face goes white, then red. "That's sure as hell not what I was led to believe. I must have gone out there to check. I must have, otherwise—" He flips through the papers in one folder, then the next, like it will give him the answers he's looking for.

"It's all right. The Hamilton Heights property is just a freak accident in terms of scheduling and visits, but I have a feeling this guy played us."

"Jesus. For another few months' rent, he let those people think—"

"Exactly."

Mike stands up, gathering the folders into his hands. "I'm going to get more information about this. If there are still tenants living there now, it's not going to look good if—"

Christine is hovering near the doorway. "Go. Let me know what you find out. Do you have a message for me, Christine?"

Her mouth is pressed into a thin line. "Not exactly."

I'm pissed off about the Hamilton Heights situation. I'm not about to back out now—not a chance in hell—but I need to know if this company is screwing me in some other way I haven't foreseen. "Then what is it?" I don't mean to snap at her, but I desperately need to get off...my ass, and get Isabella out of my head, at least for a couple of hours.

With a barely perceptible shake of her head, Christine steps aside, and the doorway is immediately darkened by another figure.

"Hi." Isabella steps forward as if Christine was never there. "I hope I'm not interrupting anything."

It's a far cry from calling me an evil bastard, and I can't help the smile that spreads across my face. "You're interrupting. But nothing that can't be rescheduled." Christine crosses behind her, heading back to her desk, and I can tell by the set of her jaw that she's not thrilled about rescheduling my meetings. Well, too bad. That's her job. "Come in."

Isabella steps further into the office, reaching out to pull the door shut behind her. My heart beats harder. We haven't made any plans for this evening yet, much less the middle of the day. I have no earthly idea what her plan is, or what she's about to do, and I relish it at the same time that I want it to be over. I want her to play her hand. I want to join in the game.

Her green eyes dancing, Isabella lowers herself carefully to her knees on the floor of my office, demurely casting her gaze to the floor as soon as her knees make contact with the hardwood.

"I'm sorry I missed yesterday." Her voice is low and sexy and I could listen to her all day. There's a strange ache in my chest at the sight of the sun in her dark hair. *I'm going to miss the hell out of this when it's over. It's going to hurt like a bitch.* I have to dismiss the thought, because she speaks again. "Is there anything you want from me now?"

CHAPTER NINETEEN

Isabella

J ASPER DIDN'T TELL ME TO COME IN. HE DIDN'T FIGHT ME ON taking Sunday for myself, either. I don't know what I was hoping for when I sent that text, but I sure as hell was disappointed when he caved. That's not the kind of thing I'd expect from Jasper. Especially not after that sweet, sweet torture he put me through at the awards ceremony.

The hardwood on his office floor isn't nearly as comfortable to kneel on as the carpet in his penthouse, which comes as no surprise. What *is* a surprise is how hard my heart is beating, the pounding traveling all the way up to my ears. That secretary is probably standing right outside the door, right now, and here I am, on my knees, pretending that yesterday was all my fault, that it was just a misunderstanding.

Yesterday was its own special hell. If I'm going to admit it, I thought that Jasper might tell me to get to his penthouse within the next half hour. I wanted a little more punishment, if that was going to take the form of any kind of orgasm. The ones I gave myself weren't nearly as satisfying.

He stands up from behind his desk and comes over to me, his footfalls sharp on the floor. His shoes have been shined recently, and the morning sunlight gleams on their surface. It's all I can see of him, and a tremble goes through my body. "Is there anything I want?"

Jasper's voice is a low growl, and I fold my hands together, locking them in the center of my lap. "Yes. Anything."

"I want you to honor the terms of our agreement."

"I *am*—" I cut myself off. Arguing with him isn't part of the game, and it's not part of my master plan, either. I need to keep him on his toes as much as possible while I figure out what the hell I'm going to do. I spent Sunday morning at a long brunch with my mother and sister, and she's clearly not taking it well that the building is now owned by Pace, Inc., no matter how much I try to reassure her. And as much as I want Jasper, I keep the drumbeat repeating in my mind: he's a cold, ruthless bastard. He deserves to be taken down a notch or three. It's my own fault that I feel this conflicted about him. But all that is for another time. "I know. I'm sorry."

"You think that's enough of an apology?" There's a smirk in

his voice, and in spite of myself my heart sinks a little. *Rein it in, Isabella. You don't care what he thinks. Getting sweet, sweet revenge is all that matters.*

"No?" I let the word come out as a question.

"No. It's not. I suggest you think of something better, if you're going to interrupt my workday for this kind of thing."

This kind of thing. I struggle to keep the smile off my face. This—all of this—is so hot I can hardly stand it, even if it is part of some big twisted game that we're both using for our own purposes.

Jasper turns on his heel and strides back to his desk.

I don't have to think about it. I already know what I want to do to him. I knew it the moment I hailed the cab outside my own headquarters.

I rise to my feet and follow him across the room. He's already seated, pretending to look at something in a folder in front of him. He doesn't look up at the sound of my high heels on the wood floor and he doesn't look up when I'm next to his desk. He doesn't look at me at all until I've knelt on the floor next to his chair.

"You've come to a quick decision."

I don't take my eyes off him. "How do you know it was quick?"

One corner of his mouth lifts in a smile that sends a wave of heat down my spine. "It must have been on impulse, showing up here without an invitation. There's no other explanation."

I drop my voice. "You don't think I had this on my mind all

day yesterday? You don't think I wasn't sorry the moment I sent that text?" I *wasn't* sorry about sending the text—I was sorry that I didn't lead him to making a decision that would have been better for me in the end. But that's neither here nor there.

"How sorry were you?" He swivels toward me.

I don't say another word. I just reach for his belt. He tightens his grip on the arms of his chair, and makes no move to stop me from undoing the buckle. Or his zipper. He doesn't stop me when I reach into his boxers, either, tugging his cock—rock-hard and standing at attention—out of his pants.

As it turns out, Jasper Pace is *hung*.

I keep the shock on my face to a minimum, but *damn.*

"This sorry," I whisper, and then I finally tear my eyes from his gaze and focus on the task at hand.

The instant I swirl my tongue over the head of Jasper's cock, he tenses. It doesn't seem like a good sign until I flick my eyes upward. His blue eyes are bright with lust, and he's looking at me like I might just be an angel descended from heaven.

I don't need any more than that to continue.

He raises a hand and works his fingers through my hair—purposely left loose today—while I lick up and down his shaft. His breath picks up, but he doesn't say a word, even when I'm certain he wants me to get more aggressive.

I let him dangle as long as I can, and then...then I get more aggressive.

He's so big that it's almost a struggle to fit him into my

mouth, but I don't hesitate for a second, working it in inch by inch. I don't stop, not even when he bottoms out against the back of my throat. Not even when I have to swallow, eyes watering, to accommodate all of him. I just keep the pressure up, inviting him to have me this way. I know he won't be able to resist. We've both been fucking with each other, but with my lips wrapped around him, he's going to have to give a little—at least on this.

With a low groan, he explodes into my mouth. I take every drop. I would do nothing less.

When he's spent, I stand up, reaching for a tissue on his desk. I pat the corners of my mouth with it, then plant a gentle kiss on his cheek—just like the one he gave me in the alcove at the awards ceremony. "I only have one question." I whisper it into his ear. "Should I come back tomorrow?"

CHAPTER TWENTY

Jasper

I SABELLA GRIPS THE OTHER END OF MY DESK, HER HANDS TIGHT on the edge. She is a living version of one of the first fantasies ever to flash into my mind about her, and the real thing? Damn. The real thing is a thousand times better than I ever could have imagined.

She's bent over at the waist, ass tilted up by the curve of her back and given just a little extra by the fact that she's wearing high heels. Her muscles tense as she struggles to stay in position, her body trembling. I have one hand on the small of her back. The other is between her legs. I have ten minutes before my next meeting, and I'm going to use as many as possible to tease her.

"God, Jasper..." She has to force the words through gritted teeth. Her hair was in a flawless bun when she walked through the door five minutes ago, but now there are tendrils escaping, falling around her face in gentle wisps. By the husky tone of her voice, we're past the part of today's battle of wills. She's not interested in being submissive anymore. She's interested in getting off.

And the power is in my hands.

Literally.

"Is there a problem?"

"How long are you going to do this to me?"

"As long as I want."

She groans, biting down on one of her knuckles. Then she remembers herself and moves her hand back into position, wrapped around the edge of the desk.

"I should spank you for that."

"Do it."

I can't stop the grin from spreading across my face. Every time I up the ante, Isabella calls my bluff. That first day in my office—was it only a couple of weeks ago?—I thought it was more irritating than amusing. At what point did I stop fighting it? I can't remember, and in this moment, I don't care. All I know is that Isabella has come by every day since Monday, unless I make other plans, and it's not strictly according to the arrangement. Yet...

"Are you telling me..." I stroke along the length of her slit again with my fingers, collecting her juices on my fingertips. "That you wouldn't mind if the rest of my office heard me spanking your bare ass?" She bucks her hips just an inch backward, as far as she can go without letting go of the desk, but I don't put my hand back between her legs. Instead, I rub my open palm over the absolutely flawless curve of her ass.

Isabella takes in a breath that could be a gasp, going still. Is she actually mortified at the thought that Christine—and possibly Mike Ford—might hear my hand connecting with the swell of her bottom, or does it turn her on?

I raise my hand, letting it hover in the air for a long moment, Isabella's breath going shallow and fast.

"You—you wouldn't." Her voice is just above a whisper. I don't know what, exactly, shakes her in these moments—I can never tell when it's going to happen—but the thrill of putting her in that place in her mind, where she's wondering what I might do, makes my cock jump against the fabric of my pants.

I lean down to growl into her ear. "Wouldn't I?" I pull my hand away again, and she tenses, her green eyes burning into mine.

While my hand is still somewhere in the air behind her, I press my lips against her neck, just below her ear. Goosebumps rise near her hairline. She twists her face up, away from the surface of the desk. The movement—the invitation, the question—makes my heart ache in a way that takes me by surprise.

I don't even think about it. I don't turn her down.

I just kiss her, softly at first, then harder as the heat between us ratchets up.

When I pull away, her eyes are still on mine, still an inferno of need and desire. But there's something else in her expression, too. Something softer. Something wondering.

I put my hand back down on the small of her back.

"You only have a few minutes left," she whispers.

No words come to mind.

All I can do is slide my hand down, tracing my fingers lightly over the cleft of her ass, making my way to her molten core. I push three fingers gently inside her, still looking into her eyes, still watching the fire burn.

I curl my fingers and her lips part an inch. The breath she draws in is nearly silent, but her eyes go wide. While she's still tensed around my fingers I pull them out, searching for her clit.

I find the swollen button and press my fingertips against it. "Spread wider."

She does, giving my hand the room I need to move. Her eyelids flutter closed, and then she opens them again. The word *please* forms on her lips. It's a soundless plea, but it's the loudest thing to ever echo through my heart.

I increase the pressure on her clit, rubbing harder, picking up the pace. Isabella's knuckles are white on the edge of the desk and the trembling in her legs has taken over her entire body. "Oh..." It's a sweet sound escaping her lips, once, then twice.

She loses control right at the bitter end, her hips bucking in spasms that she can't seem to stop, and then she explodes over my hand, another wave of juices coating my fingers. Isabella

RUTHLESS KISS

covers her mouth with her hand, her cries muffled by her palm, but she never takes her eyes from mine. I don't even have to tell her not to.

She's still panting when I sweep a tissue between her legs and tug her panties back down, then pull her skirt down into place. For once, she doesn't hesitate to take my hand, straightening up a bit unsteadily, her cheeks pink.

There's a knock on the door. "Mr. Pace?" Christine's voice is tentative, with an edge that I can't help but read as accusatory. I laugh, keeping my voice low. Whatever she's accusing me of in her imagination, she's probably right.

Isabella reaches up and puts her hair back into place, squaring her shoulders. Then she casts a look around. Her purse is on the floor near my foot, and I scoop it up and hand it to her.

She takes it in silence, her eyes searching on mine. I wait for the quip, for the last word she's sure to get in before she leaves, but instead she rises up on her tiptoes, kisses my cheek, and heads quickly for the door.

Christine has her hand raised to knock again and Mike Ford is looking in over her shoulder when Isabella pulls the door open. I can't see her face, but judging by Christine's expression, she's just given them a look that says *ask me if you dare.*

Isabella disappears through the door and Mike comes in, already talking, but none of his words land at all.

What the hell was that?

CHAPTER TWENTY-ONE

Isabella

MY MIND IS A WHIRLWIND WHILE THE ELEVATOR TAKES ME up to Jasper's penthouse. The movement of the car is so smooth, so silent, that the only indication I'm even moving is the falling sensation in the pit of my gut.

That feeling might be something else entirely.

I'm not sure.

It's been two days since that strange moment in his office, and my chest still feels tight and warm when I think about it. Why did everything go so quiet? Why did I feel like we'd suddenly made it to another level, beyond all the bantering, beyond all the fucking around with each other?

That's what we're doing, right? We're both just playing a game. Although the stakes are higher for me...at least for the moment.

I'm going to find a way to get my hands on my mother's building, and sooner rather than later. She's started calling me every couple of hours, usually under the guise of asking about something else. The conversation always turns to the building, her apartment, the fact that she hadn't planned on leaving and doesn't want to. She also doesn't want the rest of the tenants to leave. "I've known some of these people ten *years,* Isa," she told me during the fifth phone call, her voice shaking. "I'm not ready to start over."

It makes my heart ache, hearing her so upset. To some people, it might be just an apartment, but the little place in Hamilton Heights was the first time she'd felt secure in years. I know, because I spent the first night there with her. For the first time since I was a teenager, she slept through the night, late into the morning, and didn't wake up once to pace in the living room or listen near the window for any sign of trouble.

It dawned on me in the middle of the night last night that Jasper never promised me the building. He never did, and that little detail was something I should have insisted on negotiating.

But I didn't, because...

Because I wanted to get back at him for the way he underestimated me. For the arrogant way he treated me.

And because I wanted him.

I *still* want him.

The elevator glides to a stop, and my mind is still a mess. He didn't make plans for yesterday, and I spent the evening out with some girlfriends. Evie came along, too, and she wouldn't stop staring at me like I was some kind of freak show.

"What's going on with you?" She'd had to shout the question into my ear over the music of the club we went to. I needed more alcohol before I hit the dance floor, and Evie stayed with me to have one more fruity cocktail.

"With me? Nothing. Just running a successful business, trying to get three new stores up and running, dealing with Mom..."

"Bullshit." She'd pursed her lips. "What's really going on?"

"What do you think?"

"You're acting super suspicious, Isa."

I'd raised my eyebrows. "About what?"

"I've known you since you were, like, two."

"And?"

"And I was there when you started working in this business at some age that could have gotten Mom busted for breaking child labor laws—"

I rolled my eyes. "I was fourteen. And it didn't take off for at least a year or two after that."

"Don't try to change the subject."

"*You* changed the subject."

"Who's the guy?"

My heart had beat harder. "There's no guy. I'm still recovering from Jason."

"I don't believe you, especially because you're lying." My

phone had buzzed just then, and Evie gave me a pointed look. "Who's the message from?"

Jasper. "None of your damn business."

She laughed, shaking her head. "Oh, *very* convincing. I'm sold. Isa doesn't have a new boyfriend."

"He's not my boyfriend."

"So he *does* exist."

I willed the blush to stay the hell out of my cheeks. "If you must know, I am in contact with Jasper Pace."

Evie delicately put her cocktail down, then slapped both hands against the table. "I knew it." Her triumphant cry didn't even make it past the boundaries of our table, but it made my face hot. "I said you had a thing for him when all this started."

I injected all the exasperation I could muster into my voice. "I told you I met with him. We're in negotiations about the building."

"What kind of negotiations?" Evie waggled her eyebrows. "Does he ask you for favors in his office?"

"Who even *are* you?" I'd tipped the rest of the cocktail into my mouth. "Let's go dance."

"Your sister who loves you," she sang as she followed me out to meet up with the other girls. "It's just too bad you love Jasper Pace more."

Her words had sent my heart soaring, then plummeting. I am not in love with Jasper Pace. That thing between us in his office on Thursday—that was just a strange moment between two people who have been playing an intense little game for long enough to have gotten familiar. That's all that was.

Aside from all of it, I'm going to melt down completely if we don't move on to bigger and better things.

Like real, honest-to-God sex.

I'm losing sleep over it. Not that I want to tell Jasper that. But all of my nerves are molten, and I need this. It's all getting to be too much. Something has to give, and I choose sex. Sex is what has to happen, and it has to happen today.

The doors open, and there he is, standing in the lobby of his penthouse, hands in his pockets. Jasper's got his sleeves rolled up to his elbows, and backlit by the light streaming in through his living room windows, he looks...

He looks royal. He looks commanding. He looks sexy as hell.

I step inside, and something snaps. I can't wait anymore. I can't. I *can't.*

The decision isn't a conscious one—it just happens. My purse falls from my grip onto the floor, and my knees hit the carpet a moment later. I don't wait for him to address me. I don't wait for him to set the tone. The plea tears from my throat before I can stop it.

"Jasper...please. *Please.* I can't wait any longer."

CHAPTER TWENTY-TWO

Jasper

T HIS IS THE SECOND GLIMPSE I'VE HAD OF ISABELLA AT HER
most genuine, at her most raw, and if I wasn't painfully hard
already, there's no denying it now.

Saturday, just before noon, and she's on her knees in my entryway. She doesn't look quite like her usual self, and it takes me a
moment to realize that it's because she's wearing a sundress.

A *sundress*.

Every other time I've seen her, she's worn a smart skirt suit or
sheath dress and blazer or, for the awards ceremony, a gown that
took my damn breath away. I've never seen her so casual. That de-
spite the fact that the sundress isn't something cheap from one of
the boutiques in the Bronx. It's exactly the kind of sundress that
I'd expect her to be wearing—not couture, not ostentatious, but
quality, the fabric hanging delicately over her legs.

I'm at her side in an instant, lifting her chin in my hand so that she has to look up at me. There's a real desperation in her green eyes. It's so sharp, so tangible, that I'm surprised there isn't also a sheen of tears.

She raises one hand to mine, sweeping her fingers along my knuckles and then wrapping them around my wrist. "*Please.*"

Her eyes, so bright in the midday light filtering through my windows, along with the way she's breathing, her breasts rising and falling underneath the neckline of her dress, twist my heart in my chest.

I want to give her anything she asks for. I want to give her everything.

As soon as the thought comes to my mind, there's a part of me that recoils from it. An alarm blares in the back of my mind. I can't get in this deep with her. I can't get in this deep with anyone. My dad knows what the hell he's talking about. I can't throw myself in front of the same train.

I scramble for a compromise, a way to delay, but there's nothing. I know what she's asking for. I could force her to say the words, but I don't have to. I can see what she wants in her eyes.

The worst thing? I want it too.

I've been spooling this out for as long as I can, and it's been a single week. I met Isabella for the first time two weeks ago. It feels like a year. It feels like ten. She's clearly at the breaking point, and I was there with her up until a moment ago. Now I'm skidding to a stop at the edge of the cliff.

Why? What could be so fucking bad about this?

Everything.

Nothing.

I have to do something.

"Get up." It's a command, and she responds, scrambling to her feet. I offer her my hand. She takes it.

Then we're moving quickly through the penthouse, Isabella half a step behind me. I take her to the right, this time—the hallway that leads to the den, the guest suite....the master suite. My bedroom.

The master suite is at the end of the hall, taking up one full side of the building, and I push the door open just in time to keep from running into it. Isabella breathes in deep as we cross the threshold, and I throw the door shut behind me. There's nobody else in the penthouse aside from the chef, and he's on the opposite side.

My bed is on one end of the room. A fireplace in the center, sunken low so that it doesn't block the view, anchors a small sitting area. A pared-down version of my office is on the opposite side, just next to the hallway that leads to the bathroom. I scan each of the options in turn, images of Isabella in each scene flashing into my mind and back out again.

"Bend over the chair."

Isabella doesn't hesitate for an instant. She moves toward the chair in the sitting area. It's another wingback, with sturdy arms, and she positions herself in front of it, hands on the arms. She bends so gracefully that I want to take a picture. It's only then that I move toward her.

"No. This won't do." She turns her head, eyes on mine, forehead wrinkled. "Stand up."

She stands, and I go for her zipper. The dress falls to the floor a moment later.

Underneath, Isabella is only wearing a bra.

"Shoes."

She steps out of her shoes, never taking her eyes off mine.

"Fuck." I can't keep the word in my mouth, because Isabella's naked body is like nothing I've ever seen. Miles of creamy skin, all of it flawless. Breasts pert and firm. I step close, cupping one of them in my hand and rubbing around one of her nipples, already hard, with the pad of my thumb. She moans, softly, like how good it feels should stay a secret.

It's too much.

"Chair."

She turns away from me and bends, feet planted on the floor, legs spread. The folds between her legs are already glistening. "Please..." One final whisper.

I step to her side, pressing one hand firmly onto her lower back. "It's not part of the arrangement—" I keep my voice low, with a hint of sharpness. "—that you call all the shots."

She tenses. "I—"

"Quiet." I put my other palm against her ass. "All this is

supposed to be at my discretion. Under my control. And I think you need a reminder."

"Are you going to—"

"Quiet." I lean down one more time, speaking directly into her ear. "This is your chance."

She gives me the tiniest nod.

I wait.

Another nod.

"I'm going to remind you. Do you understand?"

"Yes." A whisper so soft I barely hear it.

She braces herself against the chair, and I rub idly at her bottom for another few moments. "Stay in position. Ten strokes."

I pull my hand back and deliver the first one with a *crack*. Isabella cries out, cutting herself off in the middle. I'm not going to make her count. I just bring my hand down in a relentless rhythm, Isabella trembling beneath each one, her ass going pink, then red.

When it's over, the trembling doesn't stop. At first, I think she might be crying—but she's not. She's gasping, trying to get enough breath to speak.

Her juices, gathered between her legs, trickle down the inside of her thigh.

I kneel behind her, burying my mouth in her sweet folds, and lick—one, two, three times. When I thrust my tongue into her opening, she comes so hard she screams.

CHAPTER TWENTY-THREE

Isabella

THE CAB RATTLES OVER A POTHOLE, AND I GRIT MY TEETH. I don't give a shit about the potholes. Let the car shake. At least *that* feels appropriate for the situation.

I've never been so angry in my entire life.

It took the rest of the day and the rest of the night to set in, but by the time I woke up this morning—with one message from my mom on my phone asking me when I'd be ready for brunch—I was incandescent with it.

He didn't sleep with me.

He spanked me, and he made me come with his mouth—*twice.*

And then?

And *then*?

He picked up my dress from the floor, helped me maneuver it over my head, zipped up the back, and sent me on my way.

He's not getting away with this. This is my last straw with Jasper Pace. There aren't words to describe…

There aren't words to describe how pissed off I am, and there aren't words to describe how unbelievably sexy, how unbelievably good, I felt when I stepped out of his penthouse. Yes, it hurt like hell to have him bring his hand down against my ass again and again. I've never felt anything like it—a pain so intensely pleasurable that it almost pushed me over the edge into orgasm *while he was still doing it.*

Unreal.

Absolutely unreal.

He didn't hold back. For the first time since that moment in his office, I felt like we were there together, stripped down, laid bare. And I loved it.

It felt so right that it blinded me to the fact that he'd totally screwed me over. By *not* screwing me.

I let out a bitter laugh when the pieces connected on the walk back from the gym. With every moment I sweated it out in my Lift & Burn class, my mood had darkened, which set me on edge. Going to the gym almost always has the opposite effect.

I'd stopped dead in the middle of the block when it hit me.

Oh my god. He sent me packing like…like I don't know what. He probably would have slept with a prostitute.

I spent the rest of the evening biting back my own rage and trying to breathe it out of my chest.

This is all a game, I reminded myself again and again. *You're fucking with him, he's fucking with you—it's all just some twisted way to see how far you'll both go. You know that. You've known that from the very first day.*

The same thoughts were roiling in my mind when I woke up this morning. I didn't even make it to nine-thirty before I called him.

"Isabella?" His voice on the other end of the line was tense with worry.

"I need to see you." I couldn't keep the acid out of my voice.

He'd hesitated, then let out a strange laugh. "Is everything alright?"

"It will be. Are you busy?"

I could practically picture him shaking his head. "No."

"I'll be there in thirty minutes."

I rushed through a shower—I'm not about to confront anyone in last night's bedhead—and hailed the first yellow cab to pass by, giving the driver Jasper's address, the words clipped and terse.

So here I am, my anger bursting at the seams.

The cab stops in front of Jasper's building, and I force myself to move deliberately while I pay the fare and tip the driver. I force myself to walk in measured steps toward the private elevator. I step in, swiping my phone against the scanner. Jasper installed an app on my phone that lets me access the penthouse without having to be buzzed up. The car glides upward without a sound.

He's standing in the living room when the doors open, and my heart goes crazy.

Shit.

All of the words I was going to say die on my tongue.

Jasper looks rumpled, like he might have been lying in bed. He's wearing sweatpants and a t-shirt.

"I interrupted you." About the farthest thing possible from what I was planning to say, but the sight of him makes all my plans go out the damn window. I stop at the edge of the sunken living room.

"Nope." He crosses his arms over his chest. "You wanted to see me?"

"I can't—" I start and his eyebrows go up, a new interest flashing in his blue eyes. "I need to ask you for something."

"*For* something." Jasper repeats the words carefully.

"Yes. For something."

He holds a hand out to the leather sofa and moves toward it himself, sitting down on one edge. I step down into the living room and sit in the center, not touching him. If I touch him—

I can't.

My phone buzzes in my purse and I pull it out to silence it. A message from my mom is on the screen. It starts out *You coming for brunch? I'm just so scared...*

My mind snaps into focus. This is what I'm here to do—get something out of this damn arrangement before she drives me crazy. Before I drive myself crazy waiting for something that might never happen, if Jasper has his way about it.

I look back into his eyes. His performance of being comfortable should earn him an Oscar, one arm perched along the back of the sofa. "At the very beginning of all this, you said you wouldn't force my mom out of her apartment."

"I did."

"I need more than that." There's no point in dragging this out. I bite my lip, running through all the things I could say next. I want to tell him that he's driving me slowly insane, and it might be because I'm falling for him, but I can't say that. I *won't* say that. "I need a loan."

Jasper nods solemnly. "For what? And in what amount?"

I take a deep breath, a wave of heat rising to my face. It would be one thing if I didn't need the money. It would be one thing if I had managed to work it out by now, but all I can do is rush through the store openings, and that's a recipe for disaster. And with every day that goes by, my mom loses a little bit more of her security. "I need you to loan me the money to buy my mother's building. From you. And I need it now."

CHAPTER TWENTY-FOUR

Jasper

I F THIS IS ONE MORE WAY FOR ISABELLA TO THROW ME OFF, then there's no way she can get any more devious, any more cunning.

What the hell am I going to say?

If I say yes, she's won. And if I say no, I've lost...because the moment the request is out of her mouth, I want to give it to her. I feel compelled to give it to her. There's no other way forward but to give it to her.

It's one building. In the long run, it will mean nothing to me and everything to her.

It also has the potential to end this, and end this right now.

If she doesn't need the building from me, what would she need?

And does it matter? Because the truth keeps coming in a

series of blows. I *can't* give this to her...because I need this. There's something in what we have together that makes me feel sharp and alive and part of the city and the damn planet. It's entirely new, and I don't want to give it up.

Yet...

My mind swings between the two choices like a metronome. Isabella's face is bright red, her green eyes glistening. Her lips are pressed together, the corners turned down into a little frown.

I would do anything to turn that into a smile.

It doesn't help that all the blood in my body is rushing to my cock.

She just looks so damn vulnerable. She looks, for the first time, like she needs me—she needs something only I can give to her. Her mother needs this building, and she has one way to get it. Can I really deny her that?

No. My heart beats the word over and over. No, no, *no*.

"Isabella..."

She swallows hard and blinks, a few times in rapid succession, but she doesn't break my gaze. Isabella is without a doubt the only woman who has ever been able to look me in the eye like this.

Need surges through every inch of me, from the top of my head down to my toes, a rush so powerful it sweeps me under before I can catch my breath.

I'm lunging toward her before I realize what's happening, my hands sliding around her waist, pulling her into me. She throws her arms around my neck, clinging tight and burying her face in my shoulder. I push her backward, onto the couch, and as we make contact again she arches up toward me.

"I have to have you," I growl into her ear. "I have to have you *now*."

If she answers, her words are drowned out by the pounding of my heart. I kiss the side of her neck, dragging my lips down toward her collarbone, and then I go to work on her clothes. Her tank top, the exercise capris she's wearing, her delicate bra and panties fall to the floor, and then I strip my own shirt over my head.

Isabella stretches out underneath me on the couch, her back pressed against the leather, and raises her arms above her head like she needs to brace herself against the arm. The effect sends a bolt of sexual lightning racing down my spine. Her nipples are already hard, and I lower my head to each one in turn, licking it in slow circles. Isabella closes her eyes, little moans escaping her with every breath.

For once, she doesn't have to beg.

When I'm finished with her nipples I work my way down the flat expanse of her stomach, swirling my tongue into her belly button and then working lower until I'm lapping at her clit. She spreads wide on the couch to give me access and threads her hands through my hair, guiding my head lower, urging me deeper.

A sound of pure frustration tears from her throat, and it calls to something inside me. I'm out of time, and Christ, it's never felt so good.

I move over her, wiping my lips against my arm, and cover her mouth with mine. Her lips instantly part, letting my tongue in to battle with hers, and I lose myself in it. I let the sensation of her body against mine take me over completely.

Isabella reaches down between my legs without breaking the kiss. She gives it a squeeze before she guides the head along her slick folds, coating it with her own juices before she lines it up against her opening. I push inside a fraction of an inch, and she opens her legs wider, panting into my mouth.

Then she pulls back, breathing hard, and looks into my eyes. This is her. This is all her. Nothing else. No games. No pretenses. No witty remarks. This is just Isabella at the bare heart of her.

I don't need any words to read the plea in her eyes. I'm bracing against the couch, holding myself above her, and she puts her hands on my shoulders, running them up to my jaw and back down again.

We're both still for one last heartbeat.

And then I thrust forward, filling her with one stroke.

She cries out, back arching, the sound pure, unadulterated pleasure. It makes my cock pulse inside of her, and her muscles tense around me as I pull back out, thrusting in again with a powerful movement.

It's like she was made for me.

Isabella is tight, but she's so wet that there's no resistance going in. She envelops me in her dark wetness, giving a little, stretching a little to accommodate me, and I grit my teeth, willing myself not to come. Not yet. Not *yet.*

An animal growl tears from her throat, and I have to answer it. I take her in my arms and move us both to the floor, where we have all the space we need.

Isabella curls to the side, and then she's up on hands and knees, her ass swaying from side to side as she backs up, trying to line us up so that I can keep fucking her.

I'm happy to oblige.

When I'm all the way in, the head of my cock banging against the last barrier inside of her, she grips the carpet, her fingers sinking in. "Fuck me." Her voice is husky and breathless. "Oh, *please*, fuck me."

I take her hips in my hands and pull her back against me so she can't move as I fill her again and again. "I am fucking you." I'm on the verge of losing control. "Know why?"

"Why?" The word slips out through parted lips.

"Because you're all mine, Isabella. And I love it." I pick up the pace, letting go of the last of my control. "How long are you going to be mine?" I'm pounding her with everything I have. "How long?"

"Always," she cries, and then she's coming hard on my cock, so hard I'm sure the earth is shaking, the universe must be rattled by this, and I have no choice but to give in to pleasure so intense my vision goes white at the edges.

I'm lost and found, all at once, and all I know—*all* I know—is that this is the place I never want to leave. Ever.

Ever.

CHAPTER TWENTY-FIVE

Isabella

JASPER'S BEDROOM.

We're here, but I'm not sure how we got here, or when. I'm not sure when he picked me up from the carpet in the living room—he must have, because I don't remember walking—and brought me here, my clothes still in a rumpled pile next to the couch. I wouldn't have wasted time on walking, anyway. I would have taken the hallway at a run.

The memory of being in the hallway at all is lost in a haze of pleasure.

Jasper is relentless. Just when I think there's no way I could possibly come again, he hooks his fingers inside of me, getting just the right angle for that hidden place, and my body trembles and shakes with yet another release. How many times have I forced his name through gritted teeth? I've lost count.

Satisfaction blooms in my chest, the heat there expanding and consuming me, then starting over from an ember when Jasper puts his hand between my legs again. Or his mouth. Or his cock.

The thickness of him is unbelievable. I'm no virgin, but I've never had anyone like him—not in my entire life. I had no idea this was what I've always been looking for—that stretch, that fullness, the way he takes up every available inch inside of me and then takes more.

I don't know who I've become.

I don't care.

All I want is more of him.

The light fades from the windows in Jasper's bedroom, a fiery orange spilling across the walls. That's how long it's been. I missed brunch. I'm sure there are a thousand text messages from my mother, and a thousand more from Evie, wondering where I am.

The thought is barely a flicker across my mind, because I'm pinned to Jasper's bed, my hard nipples making contact with the smooth, cool surface of his comforter. The damn thing must have an astronomical thread count. I only care about that because I'm sensitive, *so* sensitive, yet it's enough to be pressed against whatever this luxurious fabric is.

My hands are crossed at the small of my back, held in place by one of Jasper's. Stripped of his suits and his sweatpants and everything else, he's still glorious, every muscle standing out in a way that sends a shiver of pleasure down my spine every time I look at him. He's not overbuilt, but he is overpowering. He could choose not to let me get up, and I'd have no way to escape him. Far from making me feel trapped, though, the thought makes me feel...free.

Here, in his grasp, I don't have to think about anything.

I don't have to think about the building.

I don't have to think about my mom and my sister, holding some kind of weird vigil now that I haven't shown up for brunch.

I don't have to think about the buildings I'm opening, the renovations, the contracts, the money.

I'm nothing but a creature of pleasure, bent over, spread wide, my wrists held in place by the only man I've ever trusted to do something like that to me.

And why? I have no idea. But I'm not going to think about it now.

Jasper fucks me slowly, like he has all the time in the world. He fills me again and again, drawing himself out just enough so that only the head of his cock is left inside me and thrusting back in. Every nerve in my pussy is on fire with it, melting over him, another wave of release building and building with every stroke.

This is going to be the last one—at least for tonight—and it's going to be big.

My own voice breaks into the pleasure. How long have I been making that noise, somewhere between complete bliss and begging for more?

Jasper increases the pace, picking up the rhythm, and with his other hand he slips his fingers between my legs, fingertips searching out my clit. He barely has to touch me—anything more than a whisper of pressure is almost too much—and I'm rocketing toward that orgasm, that tsunami of sheer pleasure, so good it hurts.

"One more time." His voice is a low seduction in my ear. One heartbeat, two, three...and I'm coming on his cock as he goes in deep, his own orgasm taking him over, making his hips jerk against me.

It's dark when we finally move away from each other. Jasper takes my hands and pulls me upright. My knees aren't ready—they're Jell-O as much as the rest of me—and I fall against him. He gathers me into his arms, a low laugh rumbling from his chest.

"What?"

"Why did I wait so long?" he says.

I roll my eyes, even if he can't quite see my expression. "I have no idea. It was kind of ruining my life."

"Oh, I doubt that. What could *I* do to ruin your life?"

"One thing, and one thing only."

"Torture you by not having sex with you?" he teases.

"Bingo."

"I think we made up for it."

"Yes. Please don't touch me ever again," I deadpan. We both burst out laughing at that, and I step away from him, pushing my hair back from his face.

Jasper pads over to his bedside table, and his phone lights up in his hand. Then the rest of the room's lights turn on. It's a symphony of recessed bulbs and he adjusts them carefully, bringing them up slowly so I don't have to run for cover as my eyes adjust.

"You really do have everything."

He turns with a grin that has me wet. Again. After an entire day spent in his bed. Or on his floor. Lots of places, really, and I'm sure there are more in this penthouse. "I have two questions."

"I might not answer either," I drawl.

He laughs. "First, do you want to take a shower?"

"I think you've wasted a question on that. Look at me."

"I'm looking at you." His eyes flicker over my body, my nipples going hard again under his gaze. "Anyway, what's your answer?"

"Yes. *Yes.* Shower." He holds out his hand to me, and I take it with a little grin. The sweetness might be a little over the top, but I can't get enough of it. Not now.

He leads me across the bedroom and down a hallway that opens into what has to be the most upscale master bathroom on the planet. Everything is gleaming, clean, tiled to perfection, and the shower could easily fit four people in it.

Jasper steps in and turns on the water, beckoning for me to follow. The rainwater showerheads make it feel like a tropical vacation, and I tilt my head back, letting the water work its way through my hair.

"There's one more thing I wanted to ask."

I open my eyes, looking at him through the blur of the water, my core heating up. "Ask it."

"Don't go back to your place." Jasper slides his hands around my waist, leaning down to kiss my collarbone. "Stay here tonight."

CHAPTER TWENTY-SIX

Jasper

S HE PRESSES HER LIPS TOGETHER, SWEEPING HER HANDS OVER her dark hair one more time. Isabella is a vision in the water, every droplet glistening against the curves of her body. I run my palms down over her hips. She shivers, a smile playing over her lips, and closes her eyes.

"Don't..."

"Are you telling me that I can't—" I run my fingertips around the front of her hips and she twists under my hands, a satisfied laugh bubbling up from her chest.

"I'm not telling you anything."

"I beg to differ." I move my hand back to her waist. The water is just hot enough to make her skin rosy. I've had my hands all over her for most of the day, and it's still not enough. "But you don't have to convince me that you just can't take another—"

Isabella puts her hands on mine, hesitating for just a moment, then leans in, her head against my chest, the water cascading down over both of us. "This is not related to the original question."

"Isn't it?"

"Ha."

"You still haven't given me an answer."

"I'm still thinking."

"It normally doesn't take you very long to decide."

"I'm normally not coming down from a day of..." Her voice trails off, and she takes a deep breath in, lets it out, her shoulders relaxing.

"Getting well-fucked?"

I can feel her smile against my chest. "I don't know if I'd put it exactly that way. But it's accurate nonetheless."

I wrap both arms around her, curling one hand through the thick wet fall of her hair. "Stay."

"I shouldn't. I already missed brunch, and if I stay—"

Her voice goes soft at the end of the thought, and I have the sense that *if I stay* doesn't have anything to do with whether she missed brunch or not. I have the sense that staying means something to her, means something more than a game of constantly raising the ante or even an afternoon and evening of sex.

"If you stay, you'll get a world-class dinner, and world-class company for the rest of the night. You don't need to worry about clothes—I can have a selection sent up by the time you're finished drying your hair."

"You have a hair dryer, too? The amenities here are second to none."

"Damn right they are."

She pulls back, looking up into my eyes. There's a smoldering heat behind the green. I want to look into those eyes until the moment I fall asleep tonight. "I shouldn't," she says.

"You shouldn't have come here on such short notice, with such an attitude, either," I tease. "It seems to me that Isabella Gabriel doesn't care much about what she should or shouldn't do. She mostly cares about getting what she wants."

"I could say the same about you."

"That's why we're such a perfect match." I laugh, but it doesn't feel like a joke. The moment the words are out in the air, I know they're true.

Isabella narrows her eyes, a new light shining there. "I shouldn't stay. But you know what? I will anyway."

* * *

"Just don't make me eat in the dining room."

Isabella walks by my side down the hall in bare feet, the yoga pants and matching long-sleeved top I had sent up the moment we stepped out of the shower both perfect fits. I've got to tell Maryanne, my personal shopper, that she absolutely nailed it.

Somehow, in fifteen minutes, she found clothes in exactly Isabella's size that are both elegant and comfortable as hell. At least, I'm assuming they are, just by the graceful, relaxed movement of her body.

That could also be from the sex. "What do you have against the dining room?"

She makes a face. "It's so *formal*."

"There's a second living room in it."

"There's a tablecloth."

"I can have it removed."

"It's not really about the tablecloth."

I laugh out loud, and Isabella looks up at me with raised eyebrows.

"It's not. I just don't like to eat in the dining room when I unwind," she insists.

"Do you have a formal dining room in your apartment?"

"Of course I do. Or at least I would, if I were going to host a dinner party."

I laugh again. Her hair is twisted into a low bun at the nape of her neck—she opted not to dry her hair after all—and she doesn't bother to hide her grin. "You're telling me that you would create a dining room in your apartment just for a party?"

"If I ever had time to throw a dinner party that needed a dining room, I'd...rent one. The furniture, at least. I'm sure I could rearrange enough to make it work for one night." Isabella makes a beeline straight for the sofa and falls into it. "So, what's on the menu? Takeout?"

"By *world-class meal,* I did not mean takeout, no."

"We *are* in New York City."

I take my phone out of my pocket and send a quick text to Lucas. The dining room table was already set, but I'm not giving Isabella the satisfaction of being right about at least one of my dinner instincts. Lucas emerges from the hallway a moment later, a wide tray in his hands. He winks at me as he hands me the tray.

"We're good from here. Thanks for staying late. Oh—Isabella, this is Lucas, my personal chef."

He nods at her, and she beams back from over the back of the couch. "Nice to meet you, Lucas."

"Enjoy."

Then he's going back down the hall, walking fast, like he has somewhere to be. He probably does, but I've paid him handsomely enough that putting it off didn't seem like such a hardship.

I take the tray over to the sofa and slide it across the coffee table. Below us, the Manhattan skyline twinkles against a backdrop of light pollution. It's absolutely beautiful.

"Now all you have to do—" I uncover the plates, setting aside the thin silver covers. "—is choose a world-class movie to go with this meal."

"That's a lot of pressure." Isabella smiles at me, scooting

closer across the surface of the couch until our legs are pressed together.

"I trust you."

"I'm flattered."

There's a bowl of gleaming fruit pieces to go along with each of our dinners, and I lift a strawberry out, holding it in the air between us. Isabella shakes her head. "I'm *not* eating out of your hand."

"What are you afraid of?"

"That it might lead to other things."

I lean in closer, grinning. "There's only one way to find out."

CHAPTER TWENTY-SEVEN

Isabella

"ARE THE CONTRACTS THAT GOOD?"

I narrow my eyes at Angelique and wave the drawings in the air. "Do these look like contracts to you?"

She holds both hands in the air. "My mistake. The designs, then."

"If you must know, they *are* that good. I drew the first drafts myself."

"Yes, and then you had someone else fancy them up and—"

"Not a chance! I might be the CEO, but that doesn't mean I let someone else do all the creative work. Goodness, Angelique, are you looking to pick a fight?"

She grins at me from the door, then laughs out loud. I can't help but join in. My chest feels light and free and good, and it's all because of Jasper.

It feels so damn delicious that it almost makes up for the fact that thinking of him like this—thinking of him like this more and more every day—is tearing me in two.

"Seriously, the smile on your face is—" Angelique shakes her head, leaning against the doorframe. "Well, it's kind of creepy, Isabella."

I give her a dead serious expression. "Creepier than this?"

"Almost. I've never seen you look that happy about anything, much less designs."

I perch my chin on my fist. "What is it that you're hoping to get from me? A more time-consuming assignment?"

"Leaving now..." she sings the phrase, but turns back before she's fully back out of the doorway. "If you decide you want to spill about whoever's making you so happy, I'll be at my desk..."

"What makes you think it's a who?"

Angelique rolls her eyes. "They're designs, Isabella. Not even real-life chocolate cake makes you smile like that. I've been here long enough to know."

I stick my tongue out at her, and then we're both laughing, the sound filling up the room. "Oh, she's in it," I hear her say from her desk. "She's in it now." Then a sigh, and she gets her laugh under control enough to maintain some semblance of professionalism.

I turn my attention back to the designs for next season. I don't really do "winter" lines and "spring" lines, because I've surveyed my clients and listened to their feedback. They want versatile pieces that work throughout the year. Athletics is a far bigger business at this point than fashion, so that's where I've focused my resources. *I should stock the new locations with a few teaser pieces from the day to night line.* I scribble down a note on the pad next to my calendar.

The new locations, which are being gutted and reconfigured even as I sit here. The existing decor in all three of them could generously be described as crumbling '90s mall interior, which is not quite the look I'm going for with the Gabriel Luxe brand. Luxe because simplicity is a luxury.

I never thought one of my brand slogans would so neatly describe my life, but it does.

Things with Jasper aren't simple. They seem simple—especially when he's got my arms held in his strong grip, my aching nipples pressed against the cool comforter on top of his bed, and his cock buried so deep in me that it's all I can do to get a breath from the orgasms. It doesn't get much simpler than that. That's sheer pleasure.

But the rest of it?

It's a storm that rages in the back of my mind from the moment I wake up until the moment I fall asleep again.

I've over-leveraged myself with him. That's what it feels like. I'm in over my head, and I'm in over my head because I treated this like a challenge, like a game, and after that night at his penthouse, I think it's way beyond that boundary.

How long?

Always.

I didn't think about it at the time. I didn't have room in my bliss-addled brain to process what I was saying, or even what he was saying. I answered from a raw, truthful place.

Damn it, it's going to come back to haunt me.

Because that is the awful truth. Jasper makes me want to be with him for every possible moment of every single day. It's like I'm in high school again, how giddy it makes me to feel his hands running over my skin, spreading my legs...

His lips against my collarbone, his lips against my own lips, the way he takes control when the kisses get hot and powerful...

Powerful.

That's the word that makes me careen back toward my original position, which is that Jasper has the one thing that I want, and the entire goal here is to get it for myself. I shouldn't feel sorry about using his attraction to me for my own personal gain. If there's anyone on earth who deserves it, it's Jasper Pace. He's been relentless in doing everything he can to make himself the most money possible. He doesn't care about anything but his business, even when actual lives are affected by his actions. He's arrogant and ruthless, and he never lets up, not even for a moment.

I groan, covering my eyes with my hands. I can't be with him. Not in the long run. My ambition is nothing compared to his unstoppable thirst for more and more of the city.

"You okay?" Angelique is standing in the doorway of my office, a long white envelope in her hands.

"Yes. Just...working through some things." I put a smile back on my face, the giddy feeling creeping back in.

Angelique rolls her eyes at me, stepping into my office and letting the envelope fall to the surface of my desk. "Who's Jasper Pace?"

I look at her like she just beamed in from the surface of the moon. "Jasper Pace? Pace, Inc.? They've got the developments all over New York?" Developments...not travesties, like I'd usually say. The man has crept into every corner of my brain, that's for damn sure.

And I love it.

I love *him.*

I shove that thought away as hard as I can. Not in front of Angelique. If I'm going to decide to be in love with Jasper Pace—officially—I'll do it without an audience.

"Oh, *that* guy. The old one, right?"

"The son."

"A hot son?"

"Get out of my office."

She winks at me, then heads back to her desk.

I rip open the envelope and slide the packet of papers out. The first page makes my heart plummet right to my feet.

CHAPTER TWENTY-EIGHT

Jasper

"WHAT THE HELL ARE YOU THINKING, JASPER?" Mike Ford swivels around in his seat, eyes wide. We're in the middle of a meeting to go over some prospective designs for the new building purchases, and he was mid-sentence about two possible properties when my father, of all people, stormed into my office and started shouting.

I stand up. "What's this about?"

My dad looks at Mike Ford, eyes narrowed, and then looks at me. "I think you misunderstood my plans, son." His voice is taut with anger, and there are bright pink spots high on his cheeks. He's pissed. I just have no idea why.

"Is this something you wanted to address right now? I'm in the middle of a meeting."

Mike doesn't hesitate. He gathers up the folders on my desk, sweeping them into his hands with the papers in disarray, then stands up. "We can come back to this later, Mr. Pace. It's no problem." The *Mr. Pace* is largely for my father's benefit, but the older man doesn't so much as glance at Mike as he scurries out of the room, pulling the door shut behind him with the lightest touch imaginable.

I cross my arms over my chest and stare him down in silence.

He stares back, his eyes a mirror image of my own, his jaw set, teeth gritted so hard his chin is trembling. My heart pounds. It's not like him to burst into a meeting and reprimand me in front of staff members. I can't remember the last time we had an argument—not an argument of this caliber, but any argument at all regarding the business.

"You are making some very poor decisions." He's the first one to crack, and it sends a little bolt of pride up my spine. It's tempered by the fury in my father's voice. "Very, *very* poor decisions."

"You're going to have to help me understand what you're talking about." I keep my voice even, but the words are meant to bait him. I'm not pleased about what just happened.

"Of course, *son.* I'll help you understand." His tone is filled with acid. "A woman has you in her pocket, and you're selling our souls for her. When were you going to tell me?" For an instant, his face reveals his hurt. "Or, if not me, anyone in the company?" He tilts his head to the side, considering. "Maybe it's worse than that. Maybe everyone in the company is working with you on this, all behind my back."

"What are you talking about? Are you suddenly getting fed conspiracy theories by one of the homeless guys that camps out in the alley?"

"Are you going to look me in the face and lie to me?" My father's voice thunders. He's lost all control, and my gut twists.

There's another long moment, and then it clicks—his rage, his red cheeks, the accusations that I'm now controlled by some mystery woman.

My father has discovered the loan I'm making to Isabella. I don't know who told him—Cindy from the finance department, probably—but at this point it doesn't matter.

"Dad. One loan for one building is not going to cause the empire to crumble."

"That's how it starts." His mouth curls at the corner into a sneer. "That's how it starts, and before you know it, she's got everything and you've got nothing."

"Is this about Mom?"

"No, Jasper, this is about you. Why didn't you come to me about selling this building?"

"I made an executive decision."

He presses his mouth into a hard line. "You worked your ass off for those properties. For God's sake, Jasper, we had people planning for that one the moment you completed the sale. And now you're just going to offload it to some woman?"

"She's not just *some woman*."

"Oh, so it's worse than that." My father laughs bitterly. "Now my son, heir apparent of the entire company, is giving out properties as gifts to whoever he's sleeping with that week."

I take a deep breath, anger boiling in my chest, and then another, exhaling in a steady stream. I'm sure as hell not going to give my father the satisfaction of driving me over the edge, even if he's already lost it.

"First of all, you need to get your facts straight."

He waves his hand sarcastically in the air. "Enlighten me."

"I have not yet sold the building to Isabella Gabriel, who approached me with a certain interest in the property. I intend to do so, and I will, but I am not giving her any property as a gift."

My father nods slowly. "But you are sleeping with her."

The way he says it, it sounds so cheap. It sounds like a one-night stand. It sounds like I'm not in love with her, and it sends a stab of pain through my heart.

Holy shit.

I put a hand to my chest, dropping it the moment I realize what I'm doing. I might have thought it before. The idea of loving Isabella might have been blooming in my mind for the past couple of weeks, since the moment I first saw her. And it's been growing every day since. She's so alive with independence, with determination, with wit—and all of it combines to give her a fiery beauty that I'm never going to want to be without.

I have to do something about this.

On instinct, I reach for my phone to tell Christine that I'll be out for the rest of the afternoon.

"What are you doing?" My father's voice stops me mid-reach.

"You don't have to concern yourself with the company's assets." I meet my father's gaze, but an intense energy is rocketing through every inch of me, and I have to *move.* I have to move on this now. I'm done fucking around when it comes to Isabella Gabriel, and I want her to know it. "I'm giving Isabella a personal loan."

"So she can buy a building from the company?" My father laughs out loud. "You don't see a bit of a conflict there? You see absolutely no problem with paying a woman to buy one of the assets we own?"

"I'll sell it to a third party first. Is there anything else you wanted to yell at me about, or do you want to go back to your own office and calm the hell down?"

"Don't do this." My dad stabs his finger into the air at me with every word. "Don't *do* this. I don't know who she is, and I don't know what she is to you, but it's not going to last. It's not going to last, and she'll have played you for the idiot you are, and you'll be left with nothing. You won't have her, and you sure as hell won't have everything you worked for." He shoves his hands in his pocket and shrugs. "There'll be nothing left."

Then he turns on his heel and walks out.

CHAPTER TWENTY-NINE

Isabella

"T HERE HAS TO BE A WAY."

Bernadette sighs on the other end of the line. I can just see her, pressing her lips together in a little frown, her face lit by the glow of her computer. Never mind that it's mid-afternoon, and Bernadette has an office on the other corner of the building with huge windows and plenty of light. "Isa, I'm just not seeing—"

"Look again, Bernadette. Go through everything. Go through personal assets. I don't need enough to purchase the building outright. I think, if I play my cards right, I should be able to skate by with just the down payment at this point."

"Your investors—"

"Will *love* it. They'll love it, okay? Just look. Call me back when you find something."

She takes in a breath.

"Even if I don't want to hear it, Bernadette. I just need you to try one more time."

"Okay."

"Isabella."

The voice at my door startles me so much that I drop the handset. "What are you doing here?"

"Isabella?" Bernadette's voice is small and soft, coming from the handset, and I scoop it back up.

"I'll talk to you later, Bernadette." Then I put it back into the base and look back up into Jasper's eyes. He's standing in the doorway, breathing hard, like he just ran here from his own office. I know that's not what he did, but if he didn't run here at his absolute top speed, why the hell is he breathing like that? I stand up from behind my desk, searching his face for a clue. "Is everything okay? You look—"

"Isabella, I love you."

My heart soars as my gut drops to my toes. "Are you having a stroke?"

"No." He steps into the office, not bothering to close the door behind him. I'd bet everything I own—not any of my money, since I might not currently have enough of that to do a damn thing without him—but anything else that Angelique is frozen at her desk, listening to every word. "I'm not. I love you."

"You can't—"

He comes to my desk, and everything in me aches to touch him, aches to leap across the desk into his arms. But I'm frozen on the other side. I can't do anything but watch this play out. "I can." His voice is sure, firm, uncompromising. "Listen—I don't understand it. I don't understand a damn thing, but I know I've fallen for you, and I had to tell you. There was no question in my mind when I left my office that I had to tell you, and there's no question now. It doesn't make any sense." His grin illuminates his face, and everything in me goes hot. "It doesn't make any sense, but nothing about the way you make me feel makes sense, and I don't care."

I take a deep breath and let it out. "You're babbling. You're not making sense."

Then he's around the desk, both hands around my face, and his blue eyes are so intense in the golden afternoon light that the image of them, that silvery ribbon around his pupils, the blue that's like the ocean one moment and the sky the next, is burned into my mind. I'm never going to forget the look on his face right now. "We've been fucking with each other since the first minute we met." Jasper's voice is a low hum reverberating in my core. "I'm done fucking around. I want to be with you. I love you. I don't know what that means for—for the long-term, or for you. But I love you, and I want you to be mine. What do you say to that?"

I'm struggling to catch my breath. My skin is warming under his hands. I want to slam my office door shut and get out of these clothes, strip him out of his, and straddle him while he sits in my office chair. "Is this another game? Is this—is this your next move?"

A serious expression flashes across his face, and I realize it's the first time either of us has acknowledged that we *are* playing with each other. That this didn't start out as anything real, and it's become something more. "It's not a game." A grin spreads across his face. "Unless you want it to be."

"What does that even mean?" I let out a breathless giggle and clap my hand across my mouth. I'm not going to transform into the kind of woman who is always breathlessly giggling just because the sexiest man she's ever seen is inches from her face, looking like he wants to start kissing her right now and never stop.

"I want to be with you." He's clear with every single word. "Do you want the same thing? Do you want to be with me?"

I don't have a strategy for this. I don't have a plan in mind. In fact, telling him the truth in this moment will set fire to everything I've been planning for Jasper Pace. It will mean the end of my revenge plans. It will mean trusting him to do the right thing with my mother's building. But my thoughts are whirling in my head and I can't come up with a lie. I can't even come up with a witty response.

"Yes."

He leans in, and I wrap my arms around his neck. "But it—oh my *god,* Jasper, it's so fucking foolish. This isn't what I planned—"

He laughs, low and gentle. "When have we ever done anything according to plan?"

Then his lips are on mine, soft and possessive and sweet, and

I melt into his arms. My entire body glows with it, with the way he's holding me, and for once I don't second-guess anything at all. For once I don't make any devious plans. I just let him kiss me, giving myself over to him, totally and completely. I thought I'd been doing that all afternoon at his penthouse, when he fucked me to a level of satisfaction I've never experienced before and will only experience again if I can be with him.

A slow clap comes from the doorway, but it takes several heartbeats for it to register. Even then, I can't wrench myself away from Jasper, so I let the kiss come to an end naturally, slowly, while the applause continues.

Angelique is standing in the doorway, a folder in her hand, beaming at me. "That was quite the show. Is there going to be an encore?"

Jasper kisses me on the cheek and gently disentangles himself from me. Then he strolls out the door, smiling at Angelique. "You'll have to wait and see, won't you?"

CHAPTER THIRTY

Jasper

I SABELLA LIFTS HER WINE GLASS IN THE AIR. "TO ENDING THE game."

"To ending the game." We clink our glasses together, and then she dissolves into laughter for the thirtieth time since I spirited her away from her office in my town car. I never would have taken her for the kind of woman to skip out on work on a random Wednesday to spend the afternoon at a restaurant and the evening—well, that's to be determined—with me. "What's so funny?"

"I bet..." She takes a sip of the wine, a white that's so sweet it could be dessert by itself. "I bet you have no intention of ending the game."

"What game are you talking about? The game of romance?" I wiggle my eyebrows at her. "The game of life?"

She purses her lips, trying to look serious. "We did make an arrangement, of sorts."

"Oh, *that*." I take a second sip of the wine and feel the buzz travel down into my gut, mixing with the warm happiness already settling there. "No, I have no intention of ending that. You're absolutely right."

"How much time do we have left?"

"What makes you think that agreeing to be with me doesn't extend it into infinity?"

Isabella shrugs, her white teeth flashing with her smile. "All of life can't be *at your discretion* and *under your control*." She lowers her voice for those phrases, drawing a laugh out of me. "I'd never stand for that."

"Maybe you would."

"I wouldn't."

"We'll see."

I called her from the town car and told her to cancel all her afternoon appointments. I expected a back and forth, a delay, something tantalizing and infuriating, but she'd waited only a single moment before she answered. "I'll be right down."

Isabella sets her wine glass on the linen table cloth and breathes in deep, glancing out the windows at the sunny day. We're on the ninth floor, and from here you can see the hum of the city. It looks alive, glowing in the afternoon light. It doesn't hold a candle to Isabella. "So," she says, looking back at me with her green eyes dancing. "Let's talk details."

"Wow." I lean back in faux shock. "You do *not* waste any time getting down to business."

"I could say the same about you." She arches an eyebrow at me. "Details."

"What details are you fishing for?"

She rolls her eyes and laughs. "What is this going to look like, Jasper? Are we just supposed to launch ourselves headfirst into a serious relationship?"

"I get the impression we've already...launched."

Isabella considers this. "You *did* interrupt my entire workday to declare your love for me."

I lean forward and wait.

She leans back a little, looking at me from the corner of her eye.

"What?"

"Nothing." I let the word fall nonchalantly from my mouth.

I can wait all day.

Isabella's face goes red, and then a slow grin spreads across her face. "Don't hold your breath, Jasper. I'll do this on my schedule."

I reach across the table for her hand. "I'd expect nothing less."

She tugs at my hand, giving me a wicked grin. "I can't stay here with you forever, you know. I have to make one more stop at the office."

I'm on my feet immediately. "Let's go."

❋ ❋ ❋

I wait only as long as it takes to shut her office door behind us.

"Hands on the wall."

She raises her hands immediately, pressing her palms to the inner wall of her office and bracing herself.

"Spread."

Isabella doesn't hesitate, stepping her legs apart.

As soon as she does, I slide my hand under her skirt until my fingertips meet her panties. I let out a growl of frustration. This is going to require two hands. The lace comes apart in my fists and I shove the shredded remnants into my pocket.

Isabella's breathing hard, her hands still firmly on the wall.

I step closer, leaning down, my lips an inch from her ear. With one hand, I trace a path over the pulse beating underneath the pale skin of her neck, and I slide the other back up under her skirt. She's wet, and the moment I make contact with her slit she arches her back, pressing into my hand. "I think you like this."

She turns her head, her lips an inch from mine. "I do."

"I think you like it when I have you up against the wall..." I push two fingers inside of her and she gasps. "Or pin you down on my bed..." I pulse them in and out, then curl them to the front of her channel. Isabella's legs tremble. "Or even tie you so you can't move that gorgeous body of yours."

"I do."

"Why?"

I'm fucking her with my fingers, and her eyes flash with desperation. She already wants to come so badly she can taste it, and we've been back at her office for five minutes. She wanted to pick up some paperwork, check her messages—at least, that's what she said to the few people who were still at their desks when we arrived.

"Because—" She grits her teeth, taking one of her hands off the wall for a split second before she remembers what she's supposed to be doing. "Because I love being yours."

This is as close as she's gotten to saying that she loves me, too. Not that I expected her to make a grand confession the moment I showed up today. If there's anything I've learned about Isabella, it's that she's always going to confound my expectations.

I nip at her earlobe with my teeth, the gentlest bite, and she sucks in a big breath. "I can tell."

Then I'm behind her, unzipping my pants and lining up the head of my cock with her opening. She bucks her hips back against me, working the tip inside, and that's all it takes.

I thrust inside of her with all the pent-up heat that's been building all day, taking her in one stroke. "*Oh*..." Isabella has to let go of the wall to stifle her moans, blocking the sound with one of her knuckles. "Yes," she whispers as I pick up the pace, my hands on her hips, rocking her with this rhythm. And when I reach around her waist and seek out her clit with my fingertips, she says it again: "Yes, *yes*."

Yes, yes, *yes.*

CHAPTER THIRTY-ONE

Isabella

ONE CAR TRUNDLES BY, AND THEN ANOTHER, AND THEN THE road is clear. I run across and settle back into my rhythm, the morning air humid on my skin. Already humid, and it's only the middle of May. Everyone complains about the heat in the city, but I like it. It's the cold I can't stand. When I retire, I'm going to go somewhere tropical and never look back. Especially if I can get Jasper to retire along with me. Although—

I laugh, letting the music from my earbuds wash over me. Retiring with Jasper. It's far too early to be thinking about details like that, but I can't help myself.

I don't know what the hell I'm doing.

That much has become clear in the last few days.

At first, I could make all my decisions based on how likely they were to surprise him, to throw him off-balance. I got caught in my own trap, clearly, because I feel like I'm floating three feet off the ground, ready to crash back to Earth at any moment.

Hence the early morning run in Central Park.

I nod to a guy going the opposite direction and keep going. Breathe in. Breathe out.

Jasper wants to be with me.

That's the first fact to start with.

He wants to be with me, and in spite of everything that I loathe about men like him, I want to be with him, too. Am I ready to admit, out loud, in words, that I love him? I don't know. It feels a hell of a lot like love. My heart beats hard with it. My chest aches with it. I think of him the moment I wake up, and his grin is on my mind while I drift off to sleep. Even the prospect of toying with him beyond our usual banter is starting to repulse me, and that's why I got into this in the first place.

I don't want this to be about money.

That's another fact that weighs on my mind.

I don't want all of this to hinge on my mother's building, or even the fact that Jasper's wealth far outstrips my own, no matter how many buildings I intend to open across the state this year. I don't want to need that kind of assistance from him. I've never needed it from anyone else.

My phone rings in my pocket, the ringtone coming clearly through my headphones, and I reach for the button just below my ear and press to answer it.

"Hello?"

"Are you all right, Isa?" My mother's voice is tinged with worry. "You sound like you're in a wind tunnel. You sound like you're gasping. Should I call someone?"

"Mom!" I laugh out loud. "I'm out for a run."

"At this hour?" I can practically see her standing in her kitchen, wringing her hands. "Are you alone?"

"It's almost six-thirty. It's light out." I take in a deep breath and let it out. "And I'm not technically alone, no."

My mom sighs on the other end of the line. "That security service doesn't count."

"It really does. What's going on, Mom? Did you have something you wanted to talk about?" I take the curve to the left in the sidewalk, slowing my pace so she doesn't think I'm being chased.

"I couldn't sleep."

My heart aches. Back in the Bronx, my mom worked long hours and went to school, so she needed every hour of sleep that she could piece together. But that didn't always work out. A memory comes to me: her silhouette at the doorway to the bedroom late at night, backlit by the streetlight outside on the ground floor, the light filtering through the cheap curtains.

Are you still working, Isa?

A couple more pieces. I promised they'd be done tomorrow.

You should get some rest.

You should get some rest, Mom. I've got this. These two will cover groceries and electric.

Those bills haven't come yet.

But they will.

A pause. A heavy sigh.

I don't deserve this from you, Isa. I can always ask Mr. Horvath if he'll give me a break on rent. It's just until I'm done with school.

Go back to sleep. I'll be in soon.

I'd worked lots of nights like that, hands tired from the sewing, just so she wouldn't have to ask anyone else for help with the bills.

She never did go back to sleep, either—at least not until I did.

"Mom, you're not going to have to move. And if you do, Evie and I will be there to help you. You don't have to worry."

The silence tells me I've said the wrong thing.

"Mom?"

"I don't want to go."

"I promise you, it'll all work out. I am handling this."

"It's too much, Isa." Her voice breaks. "You're always handling everything. I never should have retired. I never should have agreed to—"

"You should have retired, but you should do more than that. You should enjoy your retirement. You've worked damn hard, Mom."

"Not hard enough. If I had—"

I stop in the middle of the sidewalk. "Don't go back to this."

"Back to what?"

"Don't—don't go back to second-guessing every decision you've ever made, Mom. We made it out of that apartment. We made it out of that neighborhood. And I'm going to keep you where you want to be. You don't have to doubt it. In fact—" I steel myself for the lie. "I've made some real progress on financing the building. I should be able to buy it back from the developers, and you can stay as long as you want."

"Oh, *Isa*, really?"

"Really." I smile while I say it to try to make the word sound as genuine as possible. "I just need to finish my run and get back to work, okay? Go back to bed. It's too early for you to be up."

"All right."

I finish my loop around Central Park with her words ringing in my ears, but even before I'm out of the shower, the excited warmth is back in my chest. So I have to figure out a few more things with Jasper. It's not the end of the world. More complicated, maybe...

At headquarters, I stride in with my head held high. Angelique looks at me from her desk with wide eyes. "You're on a mission."

"Damn right."

I open the door to my office.

In the middle of my desk is a big, white box tied with a ribbon the same color as Jasper's eyes.

"Angelique?"

She's instantly at my shoulder. "It came this morning, by courier. I had to give him a million forms of ID."

Heat rises to my cheeks, but I'm not going to let a box slow me down. I move quickly to the desk, dropping my purse onto one corner and picking up the box. There's a small card attached to the ribbon with two words: *Surprise! -Jasper*

I lift the lid.

I've been attending awards ceremonies long enough that what's inside shouldn't shock me, but it does.

Angelique hovers over me, looking into the box with a low whistle. "*Wow.*"

So much for keeping money out of this...

CHAPTER THIRTY-TWO

Jasper

MY LEGS ARE BURNING, AND MY CORE IS ON FIRE, BUT I increase the speed on the treadmill one more time, my feet connecting hard with every step. It's a reckless speed, almost out of control, but I have to do something to get some of this energy out of my muscles.

Otherwise, I'll be insane by the time Isabella arrives later in the afternoon.

Thinking of her makes my heart pound in a crazy rhythm that has nothing to do with reason. It's only love. The stupid, headlong kind of love that I felt as a teenager, only a thousand times more powerful. All I want is to be looking at her, listening to her voice, fucking her.

Finally, *finally,* the treadmill beeps, signifying the end of the mile, and I slam my hand down on the stop button.

Done.

I spent the morning lifting weights, music on loud in the background, and fitting in as many miles as I could. I wonder what she's doing right now. Probably relaxing in her apartment. Or, knowing Isabella, she's sneaking into the office on what's supposed to be a day off to work on something. She's always working on something. She never feels like anything is done.

We're kindred spirits, that way.

Just yesterday, when she got into work, the first thing she did was call me. I was waiting in my office for my cell phone to ring.

"Hi."

"You are just determined to make everything complicated, aren't you?" Her voice rang with truth, but there was also a hint of a laugh.

I played the fool. "Complicated? By doing what?"

"I assume this white box on my desk is from you. I'm basing that assumption on the tag. It's got your name right here."

"You got me. I sent it."

"Jasper."

"What?"

"You cannot send me gifts like this."

"Why not?"

"First of all—" Isabella sighed, but I'm positive there was a smile behind it. "This necklace is worth a fortune."

"I thought you'd like it."

"I *do* like it."

"Then what's the problem?"

"It's worth a fortune."

"Isabella Gabriel, you are the kind of woman who deserves extravagant jewelry. What if we were to attend another awards ceremony? I'd want you to have something nice to wear."

She laughed. "It doesn't have to be...you know what, never mind. Thank you for the gift, Jasper."

"No, tell me."

Isabella had dropped her voice then. "I want to be with you."

"I know. I'm over the moon."

"I don't want to be with you just because you can do things like...this."

"I would imagine it has more to do with my unbelievable sexual prowess."

Her low laugh made desire zing down my spine. "That, too. But I don't want you to get the idea that—"

"That you're just after my money?"

"Yes."

"But you *are* after my money...at least a little bit. My building, anyway."

"We'll see about that."

"That's all been decided," I reminded her, teasing. "You're mine. Your mother is safe. What more is there to do now, other than get the hell away from work and out of all these clothes?"

"How do you know what I'm wearing?"

"It doesn't matter what you're wearing. I want it on the floor of my penthouse."

"That sounds wonderful."

"Then meet me there."

"Necklace or not, I'm not cancelling another day's worth of meetings for you." She hung up while I was still laughing.

I'm walking down the hall to my bedroom when my phone buzzes on my bedside table, the vibration loud enough for me to hear it even from outside the room. I rub one of the small towels I keep in the gym across the back of my neck one more time and pick up the pace. *Isabella.*

It's an incoming call, not a text, and I snatch up the phone without looking at the screen. "Hello, gorgeous."

"Lovely." My dad's voice is dripping with sarcasm.

All the invigoration from my date with the gym drains out of me. "What is it, Dad?"

"Just calling to tell you that your secret's out. You and that woman were plastered all over the tabloids this morning."

I laugh out loud. "You think that's the first time we've been in the press?" I flash back to the awards ceremony—the way we danced around each other on the red carpet, the way she leaned in to make it look like we were in the middle of some passionate affair instead of a business arrangement, what I did to her in that alcove, how her face looked when I turned on that vibrator. Those photos made waves, too.

"I know it isn't. It's just that last time I had to look at pictures like this, I didn't know you were getting played by a gold digger."

I roll my eyes. "She's not a gold digger, Dad, and her name is Isabella."

"Oh, *Isabella.* What a beautiful name."

"Thank you."

"What has she asked you for so far?"

"Nothing."

He laughs, too hard and for too long. "Think again, Jasper. It might have started with something small, but she'll be working her way up by now, if those pictures are any indication."

I took her to dinner last night at a club, and the usual Friday night paparazzi were outside when we left. Both of us were laughing, and I swept her into my arms while we walked to the car. She upped the ante by crushing her mouth against mine, kissing me so passionately that it was like we were totally alone, back in the penthouse. Cameras flashed. I didn't give a shit. Isabella is the only woman I've appeared in public with like that in years, and I don't care if everyone knows how I feel about her.

"Or maybe it's not that," continues my dad, doing his best to sound thoughtful. "Maybe it's something she's asked you *not* to do. I'm sure it's probably something that benefits her while you take a loss. Does that ring any bells?"

"No." My answer doesn't sound convincing, not even to me.

"I see how it is. Well, enjoy your Saturday, son. I'd advise you not to fall any deeper into this trap."

He hangs up before I can answer.

"Fuck you," I say into the stillness of the master suite. The phone lands on my comforter with a muffled *thump*, and I turn my back on it, heading straight for the showers.

I try my best to ignore the icy pinprick of doubt in the bottom of my gut.

This might have been about power and money and property in the beginning, but it's not now. We've moved past that. Far past that.

Right?

CHAPTER THIRTY-THREE

Isabella

I press my hands into Jasper's chest, bracing myself. His blue eyes are shining, locked on mine, and there's a heat in his face that burns into my core. Holy *shit,* I love this. I love this so much.

I lift my hips again, drawing myself up as much as I can and lowering back down, hard, onto his cock. "Fuck." The word is a soft burst from his lips. His fingers tighten around my hips, and when I rise up again he adds his own strength to the thrust. I'm riding him like a madwoman, like I can't get enough of him filling all the space inside me, stretching me still, and it's because I can't. I *can't.*

When we're fucking like this, everything else goes out of my head, leaving behind an electric hum of pleasure. God, do I need it. There's a new fire lit under my ass these days, and it's because of that stupid lie I told my mother. I spend most of my time focusing on the fact that it's not a lie if I make it come true. I just need to do it rather quickly, before anything else happens.

Jasper's muscles tense, and he keeps me hovering above him, my pussy clinging to the head of his cock. The anticipation, even now, is so intoxicating that it sends a jolt of pure heat through my core. My head tips back, and I can't stop the moans from coming out of my mouth. I don't care. I don't want to.

"Do you want more of this?" He growls the words, his voice a dark, sultry invitation.

I dig my nails into his chest. "Yes. Give it to me."

He narrows his eyes, a possessive light flooding them. "What did you just say?"

A shiver runs down my spine. "I said, *give it to me.*"

He sets his jaw. "Wrong answer." Then he's lifting me, turning me, pressing me onto the comforter on hands and knees, his hands running over the flesh of my ass. "Who do you belong to, Isabella?"

A gush of wetness between my legs. I need *this* more than I ever will care to admit. I'm not afraid of him—not really—but I crave what he does to me. I grip the comforter in my fists. "You."

"And who decides what to give you?"

"You do." My voice drops to a whisper, my entire body already revving up for what's to come. I rock my hips backward, pressing my ass farther into the air.

I would never do this with another man. I'd never let another man do this to me. But with Jasper, it's different. Everything is different. I'm going to make everything different—tie up all those loose ends.

But for now, I'm going to get punished.

And I'm going to like it.

His hand tenses against my ass, and I go still, waiting.

The stroke doesn't come.

I groan in frustration, pressing the side of my face against the comforter, looking up at him with wide, begging eyes.

Jasper leans down, nipping my earlobe between his teeth. "I know what you're doing." His tone is all dominance. Wetness collects between my legs and starts to make its way down the insides of my thighs.

"I'm getting punished."

"You're *baiting* me." The corners of his lips curl upward in a smile, and then he's leaning in again, his breath hot on my ear, his lips hotter on the pulse just behind my jaw. "You're baiting me, trying to get me to punish you."

"So what if I am?" The sentence is breathless. In these moments, I *am* that woman, and there's no getting around it.

"You're forgetting that I'm the one in charge." He runs his palm over my back, between the cleft of my ass, and down between my legs. His fingertips move in slow circles around my clit, so sensitive already that the pleasure is an aching, desperate one. "I'll decide when to punish you." He rubs harder, and I move my knees apart another few inches. "You want it so badly that you're willing to get punished for something worse than telling me what to do."

"What's—what's worse than that?" I'm going to come, and he hasn't even spanked me yet.

"Trying to trick me into punishing you. If you want it that badly, you should just beg."

I try to scramble upward, but the pressure of his hand keeps me on the comforter. More pressure, and my nipples make contact with the surface while his hand works between my legs. "I'll beg."

"Don't move."

My fingers curl around the comforter again, bracing, *bracing*, and he takes his hand away from my clit just as I'm about to tumble over the edge into another orgasm. I groan again, the sound escaping me.

"Don't try to fuck with me, Isabella." His voice is still his dominant voice, but the sentence rings with another layer of meaning. If I wasn't so focused on getting off, I'd stop this whole thing right now and find out exactly what he means. "Don't try to trick me. I'll always give you what you need. Ass in the air."

I arch my back another inch, and his hand comes down against my bottom with a sharp *crack*. I cry out, but it's more from relief than pain. The heat from the strokes combines with the molten desire in my core and oh, fuck, oh *fuck* it's good. It's *so* good.

"Twenty strokes," he says, and I push back into them, letting them rain down on me.

When the last one falls, it shoves me off the precipice. I don't even need his fingers on my clit—I explode right then and there, coming hard, my legs trembling, struggling to hold myself upright. I'm still caught in the throes of it when he moves behind me, thrusting his length inside at just the right moment to add a second wave. I'm gushing all over him. He fucks me with an animal power, his hips jerking as he follows me into sheer, hot pleasure.

We're frozen together for a moment when he's spent, and then he wraps one arm around my waist and pulls me to the side, tumbling onto the pillows.

"Damn," he breathes, then kisses me softly on the swell of my breast.

My phone rings on the bedside table. "Damn is right." He laughs, low and soft. "Shh." I'm not supposed to be with Jasper in his penthouse. I'm supposed to be at the office. I have to head back there as soon as I finish this phone call. "It's Isabella."

"Isa? It's Bernadette. Am I interrupting you?"

Not this time. "Not at all. What's up?"

"I've found a way for you to buy that building."

My heart leaps in my chest. "I'll be right there."

But before I go anywhere, I toss my phone back onto the comforter and give Jasper's body a once-over. My entire core burns for him.

He grins at me, just once, and I pounce, straddling his waist and pinning his arms above his head.

"Right after I do *this...*"

CHAPTER THIRTY-FOUR

Jasper

THERE'S NO CHANCE THAT ANYTHING IS DEEPLY WRONG between Isabella and me—not after yesterday's getaway to my penthouse. Not a chance.

So why can't I set aside the creeping doubt that grows a little stronger with every quiet moment?

When she's with me, I don't see anything but her fire, her determination, her incredible wit. The way she looks at me with those big green eyes, begging for me to dominate her one minute and teasing me the next, is all I need for the rest of my life. At least, that's what I think...until she's gone, and my dad's words start ricocheting through my brain.

I'd advise you not to fall any deeper into this trap.

It's not a trap. Isabella isn't doing this to try and fuck me over.

Can you really be sure about that?

The nagging thought follows me while I throw myself into a workout at the gym, shower, and head in to the office. I have big plans for today. Mike and I are going to decide on at least one of the properties that he's located in the past couple of weeks, and I'm going to swing by the three new buildings—including Hamilton Heights—so we can discuss how the preliminary plans are going to proceed. Mike always rolls his eyes at me when I insist on doing this for all the new properties—he thinks my time is better spent meeting with investors—but I do plenty of that in the evenings, at exclusive dinner events and parties.

There's nothing wrong with wanting a little more detailed control when you're taking over real estate one building at a time. The rest of the world is going to be like New York for me soon. I'll have all the hottest properties, and with people like Mike on my team, I'll be able to find them at rock-bottom prices and make a killing.

I sigh when the town car pulls up next to the curb.

These plans just don't have my heart racing like they used to. The only thing that does it for me now is Isabella.

That thought stops me dead in the middle of the sidewalk, between the car and the building.

I can't let that happen.

Isabella can't be the only thing to excite me, to make me want to get up in the morning. Pace, Inc. has been my life since I graduated college, and I'm not willing to give it up. So why the hell do

I just feel resigned to the work I have today instead of humming with bloodlust for the next deal?

It's an off day. That's all this is. I'm still just as invested in Pace, Inc. as I was three weeks ago, before she ever came into my life.

When the elevator doors open, I step out with a smile on my face, ready to get on with this. Meetings. Plans. Expansion. The excitement will come later. I'm sure of it.

I greet everyone I see, as usual, and I'm a moment away from poking my head into Mike's office to see if he's ready to get started when he rushes out, head down, his mouth set in a line. He's so focused on getting wherever he's going that he doesn't see me.

"Whoa. Where's the fire?" I put both hands up to stop him, and he skids to a dead halt in the middle of the hallway.

"You're in early." His voice is terse, almost monotone. I raise my eyebrows, and he puts a hand to his forehead. "I'm sorry, Jasper. That was out of line."

"I *am* here early, but not that early. What's going on?"

He flicks his eyes around him like the walls have ears, then beckons for me to follow him back into his office. I shut the door behind us.

"I think we have a problem with your father."

We? If there's anyone who has a problem with him—at least at this moment, it's me. What the hell could Mike have to do with that? "What kind of problem? Last I knew, he was starting to back off a bit, heading for retirement. Don't spread that around. I'm just not sure what—"

"He's pushing the Hamilton Heights property, and the other two you signed on in March. Wait—" He opens the folder and shuffles through the papers in his hand. "No, not all three. Just the ones from Brilliance." Mike looks up at me, his forehead wrinkled from the stress. "I've been looking into the guarantees he made, and the leases, and trying to figure out what the hell happened since you first brought it up. I didn't even know he knew—" Mike shakes his head. "That's not important. Last night when I was packing up to leave, he came in here and told me there was no more time to waste on these, and that he'd sent new notices to the tenants there. He wants them out by the end of the month, not by the end of August."

"He can't do that."

"*I* know that. But the people who live in the Hamilton Heights building might not."

Shit, shit, *shit*. What the hell is my father thinking? I don't want to keep Hamilton Heights—it's not worth the hassle with the tenants.

Or Isabella.

No. Not Isabella. I can't let her affect my decisions like this. Not at work. Not now.

"Did you ever get any information about the Spanish Harlem building? What about the tenants there?"

"I did. They're still there, but all the leases end on the last day of May. It's not as much of a problem."

"It's still a pretty big fucking problem."

"Yeah." Mike nods, his expression grim. "I'm digging in today to make sure he has absolutely nothing to do with any of our past or prospective purchases."

"Where are you going right now? You looked like you were in a pretty big hurry."

Mike meets my eyes, but I can tell he's uncomfortable as hell. "To your father's office. He wanted to rush forward with starting renovations on the Hamilton Heights property even if the residents put up a fight—which they should, because they're well within their rights."

I take in a disbelieving breath. My father has no reason to get involved in this, other than to—I don't know, teach me some lesson about women like Isabella Gabriel. It's true that if he can force out the current tenants and flip the building, we'll get payoff from it much sooner.

There's a sickening twist in my gut when the realization hits. I would have done the same thing, not too long ago. I might have even done the same thing now, if it weren't for Isabella. She's willing to do just about anything to help her mother—and by extension the rest of the people in the building. I haven't even taken the time to find out what kind of community they've established, what they already offer the neighborhood…I was willing to bulldoze the entire thing to grow my empire.

I give Mike a nod. "Thanks for telling me. You should get over there. He's probably got the architect waiting. Just sit in on whatever this meeting is. Give him your two cents."

"Okay." Mike turns to go, his shoulders sagging.

"Mike."

"Yeah?"

"You did the right thing. I'll figure out what the hell he's up to."

He smiles, his lips still pressed together, like he's not quite convinced. Then he's gone.

CHAPTER THIRTY-FIVE

Isabella

M Y HEART IS POUNDING SO FURIOUSLY THAT BERNADETTE'S words make no sense whatsoever.

I couldn't sleep last night. By the time I got back to the office—probably with Jasper's scent all over me, but I hadn't wanted to stop for a shower—Bernadette was gone.

"Where did she go?" I shouted at Angelique.

"Her son's final track—what do they call them, when it's track and field? Tournaments? Meets?"

"I have no idea," I'd grumbled. Bernadette should have at least left a note, but she probably knew that whatever explanation she left in writing would also need to be talked through.

"She said she'd be in first thing tomorrow."

"She's always in first thing."

Angelique gave me a look. "I know things are moving fast, Isa, but it *is* after five."

I waved my hands in the air. "I know. I *know*." Yes, I expect a lot from my staff, but I also try not to be a tyrannical bitch. It's not a good business model. "I'm fine. Why are you still here?"

She grinned at me. "Bernadette wanted to make sure someone was here to...intercept you when you came back."

"She knows me too well." I took in a deep breath, squaring my shoulders. "You should head out. This is just a normal Monday."

"*Sure* it is." She grabbed her purse from her desk. "Walk you out?"

I opened my mouth to say that I had a few things to finish up, but who was I kidding? I wasn't going to be able to focus on a damn thing until I could talk to Bernadette.

And now, the next morning, Bernadette is talking and I can hardly take it in.

"Okay. Wait a second." I take a deep breath, close my eyes, and push all the other thoughts out of my mind. "Take me through this one more time."

Bernadette flips patiently back to the first paper in the stack on her desk. "The newest appraisals came back from the storefronts. It will take some doing, but you should be able to leverage the equity you've gained from the appraisals, which were higher than I expected, to purchase the building in Hamilton Heights."

"I have the money?"

"You have the money *in a sense*." She shakes her head. "I

wouldn't do this, Isa, unless you're absolutely sure these store-fronts are going to be in the black sooner rather than later. There is nothing left—no wiggle room—if you do this."

I give her a sly look. "That's what you said about these build-ings, and look—wiggle room." She exhales sharply through her nose, and I back off. "I know, Bernadette. I know. But the situa-tion with—" I almost slip up and say *Jasper*. "—the situation with my mom has recently become pressing. This is the best option."

Bernadette closes the folder and folds her hands on the table, looking me squarely in the eye. "Are you sure about that?"

"About what?"

"About purchasing this building. You're positive she wouldn't be willing to consider moving to a different location? Maybe somewhere closer to your place?"

I think of how hard my mom fought to move out of her old building. She couldn't stop smiling when the super handed her the keys to the place in Hamilton Heights. The first time she stepped across the threshold and flipped the deadbolt behind her, she cried tears of joy. "Oh, Isa, it's perfect." It had been the perfect day, too—uncharacteristically cool for August, which meant she could throw open the windows for a nice breeze. "I never want to leave this place. Not until I have to go into a home."

It would be a hard sell, convincing her to leave her victory apartment just to be closer to me. I'm not home often enough for it to be worthwhile for her, and Evie works constantly, too. She needs her neighborhood.

"I really don't think so." Even if I could convince her, it's going to be June before we know it. If my mother ever leaves her apartment, it won't be a season-long discussion. I anticipate it taking somewhere in the order of years.

Of course, if I don't pull off this purchase—and if Jasper goes back on his word—I might only have the rest of the summer for it anyway.

"Okay," Bernadette gives in, but I'm lost in thought again. Jasper could go back on his word. Or I could sign the papers and accept his loan. Even that seems less feasible by the day. I don't want to take his money and launch some complicated plan to buy the building from him. I just want to do it myself, like I've done everything else in my life. "I'm behind you whatever you decide, Isabella. I just want you to be aware of the risks."

I reach out and pat her hand. "I know, Bernie. You've never let me down." Then I stand up from my seat and take the folder. "I have some phone calls to make."

I'm outside the door when Bernadette swivels back to her computer. "She is just unstoppable," she says in a soft voice, almost under her breath. She must think I'm out of earshot.

You're right about that.

I make a beeline for my office. Angelique looks up at me from her desk. "I'll hold your calls."

"You really get me," I tell her, and then I'm closing the door behind me. Behind my desk, I take one steadying breath and dial Jasper's office number.

"Mr. Pace's office." I'd recognize that voice anywhere—and it's not Jasper's, it's his executive assistant Christine's.

"Hi, Christine. This is Isabella Gabriel, calling for Mr. Pace."

"Hi, Isabella!" Her tone is almost too chirpy, but that's better than terse. "He's not in right now, unfortunately. Can I take a message?"

"Do you—" Jasper didn't mention being booked for the morning, but then again, I'm not his executive secretary—why would he? "You know what, I can call back later. Thanks, Christine."

I hang up, drumming my fingers against the surface of my desk.

I don't want to wait until Jasper's out of his meeting. Or wherever he is.

I'm probably rushing into this, but maybe it would be better if I went through official channels at Pace, Inc. It'd be more professional to deal with his people directly. After all, it's not Jasper who's going to do all the legwork to sell me the building, when he does.

I search for the main reception number for Pace, Inc. and dial again. It takes two transfers, but finally a man named Lowell picks up the phone.

"Lowell Wexler, Head of Real Estate Acquisitions."

"And sales, too, I hope."

He laughs, his voice deep and rich. "I understand I'm speaking with Isabella Gabriel. I've seen you in the press lately." My stomach tightens at the sly tone.

"I'm calling because I wanted to speak to someone directly about purchasing one of your properties." I cut right to the chase. No more time to lose.

"Which property were you interested in? I know Mr. Pace and his son haven't been interested in selling for some time, but I'm happy to look one up for you."

"An apartment building in Hamilton Heights." I give him the address.

I can hear his fingers on the keyboard of a computer. "Hmm. Oh—that's a recently acquired property, Ms. Gabriel. Pace, Inc. won't be looking to make a sale on that building until after the development has been completed. And it looks like it's slated to begin rather soon. You might do better to call back in a few months."

"Yes, I realize that, but—wait, how soon?"

"I'm sorry I couldn't help you, Ms. Gabriel. I'll pass along the message that you called."

Then, before I can get another word out, he hangs up.

CHAPTER THIRTY-SIX

Jasper

MY HEAD IS THROBBING WHEN I STEP OUT THE FRONT doors of Pace, Inc., but with every block the town car gets from the building, the pain lessens.

So today was a shitty day, and my dad is becoming unhinged in his old age. Mike Ford reported back that he's had the design team working all day on a new set of designs to replace the ones I've already looked at for Hamilton Heights. I don't know what he thinks he's doing—at some point, he's going to have to talk to me directly about it—but it's enough to make the muscles at the back of my neck feel tight and tense.

Isabella is the solution. She always is.

But when I get to the penthouse, she's not there.

As soon as I open the door, the ringing silence confronts me.

I told Lucas not to come in for another hour to start preparing dinner because Isabella was supposed to meet me right after the office. I've been fantasizing about her ever since I got in the car. I was convinced, until I opened the door, that she'd be kneeling on the carpet, those flashing green eyes on the floor, her lips parted in anticipation. She's been ready for me every single evening since last Wednesday, when I rushed into her office like a lovesick teenager.

Something's off.

I send a text to her phone.

Working late? :)

The smiley face is a last-second addition. Something probably did come up at work—it's not like I expect her to shelve her ambition just to have sex with me as soon as humanly possible every day—but I don't want her to think I'm watching the clock, waiting for her arrival.

Even if that's exactly what I'm doing.

When she's not there after fifteen minutes, I head to the master bathroom, strip off my clothes, and take a shower. She'll undoubtedly be here by the time I'm out.

I take my time toweling off and choosing a button-down and pair of shorts, but there's no alert on my phone that the elevator is incoming, no soft whirr of the machinery as it lifts the car up to the penthouse.

When the doors do open, it's to reveal Lucas, who is surprised to see me in the living room.

"Mr. Pace, hi. I thought—" He presses his lips closed, reddening slightly.

"It's Jasper to you." I put a jovial smile on my face. "Don't mind me. I'll just be…doing my thing." It sounds awkward and strange, but Lucas just nods and disappears down the hall.

A twinge of worry settles in the pit of my gut and starts a slow bloom. Not only is Isabella not here, she's also gone totally radio silent. It's not unlike her to take a while to answer—she gets immersed in her projects like I do—but after the weirdness with Mike Ford in the morning, my father's endless meetings all day, and that snarky comment he made about *things she'd asked me not to do*, everything is taking on a sinister tone.

I rub my hands over my face. For all my dad's bluster, he hasn't made it far with the new plans he's intending to carry out on the two buildings from Brilliance. The one thing that's going to be a problem is when Isabella's mother gets notice that he's going to try and force everyone out in less than two weeks.

I should have called her about that, given her warning, but I bet the letters won't arrive until tomorrow or Thursday. I still have a chance to smooth out the whole thing, even if that means I have to go to the property in Hamilton Heights myself and assure people that the letters are the act of a madman and not Pace, Inc.'s actual wishes.

The call comes in just after seven, and I answer on reflex. It's probably Isabella. She's probably so sorry about working late, and she's probably on her way right now.

"Hello?"

"You'll never guess which charming creature just came to meet with me." My father's voice is ringing with satisfaction.

"Dad." It's all I can do not to sigh out loud. "Don't call me with this bullshit. I get that you're pissed off, and we can talk about that at the office tomorrow, but it's been a long day and—"

"Your little girlfriend."

The words make my stomach recoil, but I take another breath in and let it out. "I sincerely doubt that Isabella wanted to meet with you. She doesn't even know you."

"She does now. We've been getting to know each other over the past few hours, working out a deal."

"Involving?" My head is starting to ache again. What the hell is this man's plan, and why did the potential of one personal loan, combined with an easy sale for Pace, Inc., make him react this way?

"That property in Hamilton Heights. You're not going to believe it, son. I sold it to her for a wonderful profit. Not as much as we would have made from developing it, but I'm happy to be rid of that lingering issue with the tenants."

My mouth drops open. "Are you joking? You're the one who wanted to move forward with that property. You wanted to force them out early."

He chuckles like this is a fun prank between friends. "I did. I really did. And I had that letter drawn up in haste. I was able to stop it from being sent, though. Now it's not our problem. Aren't you thrilled?"

I'm not fucking thrilled. I'm confused. I'm torn. On the one hand, Isabella has what she wanted—but she didn't have to go to my father for that. She was going to get it all along.

On the other hand, he was right.

It dawns on me slowly as my dad goes on about the arrangement, how closing shouldn't take much time at all, how he's happy not to have to micromanage this project. How, if I'm going to be influenced by women like her, I may not be ready to step in after all. None of it registers.

Because she used me.

I used her, too. I used her for pleasure, but when I fell for her, I stopped fucking around.

She didn't.

And now I don't know which things were true and which were lies. She had the money all along, so what else did she say just to get what she wanted?

He was right.

Fuck.

It was a game until it wasn't, and now, suddenly, I'm standing on the other side while it's revealed that yes, after all, it *was* a game. It was a waste of time.

My heart goes cold.

"I have to go, Dad. We'll talk about this later." I hang up, and my phone vibrates in my hand. The elevator is on its way.

It has to be her.

Then the doors open.

CHAPTER THIRTY-SEVEN

Isabella

AFTER THAT MEETING, I NEED TO SIT DOWN WITH A GLASS OF wine—maybe two—and fit my head around everything that just happened.

Naturally, I was not one to sit down and take the brush-off from that Lowell asshole, but when I called back a third time, Jasper was still out.

I stewed all day, waiting for my cell phone to ring, but it didn't. Either it was one long meeting or Jasper was avoiding me—who the hell knew? In the end, the urge to move forward was stronger than the desire to play the part of the cool, collected professional one hundred percent of the time.

So I went to the Pace, Inc. building. I waited as long as I could.

My heart was in my throat as I took the elevator up to the

floor with the executive offices, a giddy triumph rising in my chest to eclipse the nervousness that had been building all day.

But Jasper wasn't the one in the hallway when I stepped through the doors.

It was empty except for an older man, silver haired, wearing an impeccable suit, and a younger man in a shirt and tie, the shirt looking slightly rumpled. They were standing together, heads bent over a folder. I tried to move past them, but the older man lifted his eyes, a broad, familiar smile on his face.

I returned the smile. "You must be Mr. Pace."

"And you must be Isabella Gabriel."

I extended my hand for him to shake, forcing myself not to show any suspicion in my face. "I don't think we've met before."

"Not in person, no." The senior Mr. Pace leaned in, a twinkle in his eye. "But I've read about you in the press. Your business is growing quite quickly, isn't it?"

There was an article in Forbes not long ago about Gabriel Luxe, but somehow it surprises me that this man would have any interest in a fashion company. "I have big plans for expansion."

He'd chuckled then, as if it were a joke. "I'm sorry to disappoint you, Isabella, but my son is downstairs in an investor meeting. Is there anything I can help you with, beyond leaving a message?"

It was reckless, in retrospect, but I felt ready to burst, ready to implode if I couldn't take at least a single step toward buying the damn building. "Actually, there is."

"Come on down to my office. Mike, sit in on this, would you?"

That's how it started, and by the time I left—well after the time Jasper and I had arranged to meet at his penthouse—I'd signed a preliminary agreement to buy the Hamilton Heights building pending approval from my financer. Bernadette is already in contact with our man at the bank. Full approval should be done by Friday, with a push on the timeline because his wife loves my clothes. I'm willing to give the woman an entirely new wardrobe if that's what it takes to get this done, so I can move on from this with Jasper and into a life that doesn't hinge on me being a damsel in distress.

My heart is in my throat on the elevator ride up to his penthouse. I didn't text him when I got into the car. I should have, but the last thing I wanted was to have to explain in tiny text chunks the incredibly bizarre meeting I'd just had, even if it did end in triumph.

He's probably not going to be thrilled about it, but at the very least, there's going to be dinner. I won't mind if we retreat to the bedroom for a while before we eat. That would be more effective than wine at helping me unwind. It'll be the first time since all this began—can it really be only a few weeks?—that there will be no strings attached.

My chest goes warm at the thought of it. Now that the hurdle has been jumped, I'm free to figure out what the hell makes me so in love with Jasper.

I grin, alone in the elevator. I'm in love with Jasper Pace—every arrogant, cocky, relentless, funny, generous, protective inch of him.

The elevator glides to a stop.

The doors open.

The warmth in my chest shatters in a burst of ice.

Jasper is standing in the lobby, and this isn't the look of a man who might want to playfully spank me. His blue eyes are sharp, cutting, and though he's wearing shorts and a button-down he looks so poised to explode that a full-body shiver cascades from my head to my toes.

"Jasper—" I start talking without knowing where I'm going with this, just to try to heat the silence. "I'm sorry I'm late."

He smiles. It's not a kind smile. "I'm not sorry."

"You're not?" I step off the elevator, but there's such an undercurrent of rage surrounding him that I'm afraid to get any closer. I give him a halfhearted smile, in case this is the setup for—I don't know, rushing off to the bedroom?—but the expression on his face doesn't change.

"Not in the least." He takes a big breath in, crossing his arms over his chest. "I'm relieved, actually. This solves many problems for me."

I swallow hard. "What kinds of problems?" I'm keeping my tone soothing and low, because I have no idea what's going on here. Yes, it was strange as hell that his father met with me and caved to me like that, but I was hoping to get some kind of explanation from Jasper.

"For one, I don't need to continue wasting my time on you. Not after today."

My mouth drops open. His words register—he couldn't be clearer—but what the fuck? My stomach twists into a painful knot. "What *happened*?"

He laughs, the sound bitter and cruel. "Don't play dumb with me, Isabella. You know exactly what happened."

"I really don't." Does this have to do with the meeting? The papers are burning a hole through my purse, and I'm desperate to know what all of this means, but it's clear that I'm not going to get an answer if Jasper is reacting like this. My hand trembles around the purse's handle. Less than a week ago, he was confessing his love for me, eyes alight with it. And now?

"Let me refresh your memory. You're coming here right now from a meeting, are you not?"

"Yes."

"And who was that meeting with?"

"Your father." The ache spreads into my chest, along with a spike of anger. He doesn't have to be such an asshole. "Why are you acting like this?"

Jasper raises his eyebrows in exaggerated surprise. "*Me*? Why am *I* acting like this?"

"That's what I just said. Do I need to find you some kind of hearing aid?"

He laughs again, and somehow, it's even worse than before. "Oh, good. Try that act on me again."

"I'm not acting. I'm...fucking frustrated, Jasper, and hurt."

"That makes two of us, doesn't it?"

I shove my rage deep down, grasping for a last shred of calm. "Why don't you just tell me why—"

"Fuck that," spits Jasper. "Why don't *you* just tell me why you've been using me since the first day we met, like some kind of gold-digging bitch?"

CHAPTER THIRTY-EIGHT

Jasper

ISABELLA'S FACE HAS GONE WHITE, WITH BRIGHT PINK HIGH ON her cheeks. When the accusation lands, she sucks in her breath like I stabbed her.

"A gold-digging bitch." She throws the words back into my face, and hearing them in her voice—and echoed again and again in my own mind—makes me feel like a fucking monster.

But backing down doesn't seem like much of an option. Waves of rage are thundering off of her, and it raises the hairs on the back of my neck. I raise my hands in the air again. "Maybe that wasn't the kindest choice of words." My voice sounds like someone else's. "But the general idea applies, don't you think?"

She laughs, the sound cutting me to the core. "*I'm* a gold-digging bitch. What does that make you, Jasper?" She shrugs, looking up at the ceiling like she's really considering it. "It's true—you don't make your money from dating rich women. No, you just go around the city like it's your own personal whore. Everybody should move out of your way if you want to, say, gut a building and throw out all the tenants, right?"

"If that's what it takes." The words are coming out faster than I can stop them. It's like being on a runaway train. I can't stop, can't reverse directions, and the pain boiling in my chest is blinding me to any of the words I could use to talk us both down from the ledge.

"See? That's what I thought." She smiles at me, shaking her head a little. "I knew that about you the moment I walked through your office door. You have a reputation in the city for being a ruthless bastard, and that's exactly what you are."

"It's taken me a lot further than being a lying—"

Isabella cuts me off. "I'm sorry if I've hurt your delicate feelings by having enough money to do what I want. It must really gall you to not be the end-all, be-all for a woman."

I roll my eyes. "If I gave a shit about impressing women, I wouldn't stop at the miserable show I gave to you."

She narrows her eyes. "You didn't give me much, that's fucking true." Then she takes in a big breath and lets it out again. "This conversation is obviously going nowhere." She adjusts her bag on her shoulder and turns around, stabbing the button for the elevator with one finger. The doors slide open. Her jaw works. "I'd say I wish you the best, but—" Isabella lets out a short laugh and steps inside.

I'm lunging for the elevator before I can stop myself, slapping one hand against the doorframe. Isabella doesn't flinch. She just glares at me, and the fury in her eyes, along with a whirlwind of hurt, is a mirror image of the awful feeling taking over my entire chest, my entire body.

I just can't let her leave without an explanation.

I can't.

It'll haunt me for the rest of my life, and with every pounding heartbeat, I can feel her shutting down, drawing away from me. It's sickening. "*Why*?" I throw the word at her feet. "Why, Isabella?"

Her mouth twists. The expression shifts between a sneer and a woman trying desperately not to cry, and it breaks my fucking heart. I want to take that last step, take her into my arms, and tell her that this isn't worth it, that we can figure this shit out, whatever it is, but I'm locked in place.

"Why what?" Isabella's voice is a whisper stretched to its breaking point.

"Why did you have to lie to me?"

"Why did you have to be such an unholy prick?" Isabella's eyes are bright with tears—there's no mistaking them now—but she doesn't let a single one fall. "It wasn't my idea to start this—whatever this fucked-up arrangement is. You're the one who threw it on the table, and I know you did it just to fuck with me."

"Maybe in that moment." I hate the desperation in my voice, hate the wild hope that's rising in my chest. If we can get past this, if we can just talk—

"So you admit it. You admit that you've been playing with me this entire time."

"Isabella, you wanted to negotiate." I can see her now, leaning toward me, eyes glowing with possibility while she hinted and insinuated, an electric tension humming through the air between us. Yes, I fucking wanted her, and she wanted me. "I never expected you to—" I have to work to unclench my jaw. "I never thought you'd take me up on that outrageous deal. And when you did—"

"I signed up for this? Is that what you're saying?" She shifts her weight, standing tall. "Yeah, Jasper, I did. I took your deal, and I did it just to show you that you're not in control of everything, even if you think you are. I did it knowing that one day I'd be back on top and I could show you just how utterly useless—" She stops, shaking her head. "You can be pissed at me all you want, but you used me as much as I used you. *That's* what happens when you treat people like shit. Eventually, it comes back around."

"At least you got what you wanted." I sound fucking pathetic, and loathing rears up in my chest, adding a terrible layer to everything else.

"Tell *me* one thing." Isabella's voice goes soft, though it still has a sharp edge. "How far were you going to take this, in the end?"

The elevator door tries to close, and I push it back with my hand. "How far? Not as far as you were, obviously."

She laughs. "Buying a building from your company is going farther than telling a woman you love her? Just to fuck with her?"

I'm so furious, so heartbroken, that my teeth are locked against one another. It takes all the effort I have just to speak. "That was real. If you can't see that—"

"It's not a matter of what I see." A single tear slides down Isabella's cheek, and she wipes it away with a furious flick of her hand. "Even if you're suddenly telling the truth, I have no reason to believe you. And I'm sure—" Another bitter laugh. "I'm sure you feel exactly the same about me. We played the game, Jasper. We both fucking played the game, and maybe we both lost. But I can't do this anymore." She takes a long, deep breath. "Now, could you just step back? I'm trying to leave."

CHAPTER THIRTY-NINE

Isabella

THE BLAST OF HEAT FROM THE BLOW DRYER TAKES ME BY surprise, even though I'm the one who aimed it at my own hair.

Everything seems like a horrible surprise lately.

I get myself back together—at least enough to do my hair—and aim the dryer back at my roots. Ten minutes later, I'm staring at it again like it's some kind of foreign object. What was I even doing?

Right. My hair. My hair is dry.

It's a small miracle that I make it to the office fully dressed and presentable enough that nobody in the lobby gives me a second look. On the elevator on the way up, I close my eyes, steeling myself for another day without him.

What the fuck happened? It must be the thousandth time I've had the thought since Tuesday, and probably more. Three days and all I can do is dissect that conversation, which went wildly off the rails almost from the moment it started.

Should I have stayed?

Did I do the right thing by leaving?

My mind swings between the two options on a moment-by-moment basis. It's a torturous circle: just when I've decided that leaving was the right thing to do, I'm knocked back into indecision by the fact that my entire body aches for Jasper. My entire soul aches for him, and that's something I never thought would enter my mind.

I sure as hell didn't expect for everything to come crashing down when I got on that elevator.

Even now, getting on any elevator sends my stomach plummeting to the floor, which makes no sense.

I brace myself when it glides to a stop at Gabriel Luxe's floor.

"What are you so scared of?" I whisper it in the empty space. It doesn't help.

The doors open.

Bernadette is standing by the main reception desk, beaming.

I can't wrap my mind around it. What is she smiling about? What on earth could she have to be happy about? What could anyone have to be happy about, now that I'm so shattered?

A wild laugh bubbles up in my chest. *Self-centered much, Isa?* The rest of the world is moving on. It's just me stuck in this rut, and I'm going to get out of it, starting right now.

"Do you—" The words stick in my throat, and I force a smile onto my face. "Do you have something to celebrate this morning, Bernadette?"

"We both do." She gives me a meaningful look. "You're going to want to make a couple of calls once I tell you the news."

Her words filter in like they're coming from the surface and I'm underwater. "Calls?"

"To your mom, for one thing."

Am I pregnant? It's an absurd thought, that Bernadette might know before I do, but I have no earthly idea what she's talking about. None whatsoever. I blink at Bernadette, doing my best impression of a woman who knows what the hell is going on.

Bernadette can't keep it in anymore. "It's a go on the Hamilton Heights building, Isa. I got the news a few minutes ago. The purchase is going forward. I just need to send over a few pieces from the inventory for his wife." She winks at me, then lets out a laugh that I try unsuccessfully to echo. "I know it's early, but I've got mimosas in my office. Let's celebrate!"

I knock three times at my mom's door, trying to figure out what the sound coming from inside is. It's loud and a little on the raucous side, and I can't identify it until the door cracks open and my mom peers out. "Isa! What are you doing here?"

She pulls the door open, and the sound spills out into the hallway. It's some kind of high-powered salsa music. "Mom! You're sweating."

"I'm working out!"

"Working out?" This does not compute. My mother has never had time in her life to work out.

"Evie suggested it to me. Come in, come in." She ushers me into the living room, where the workout is still in progress on the television. "She brought me a DVD player and three of these videos. To keep me thinking positive."

Evie would suggest exercise, because that's what she does for herself when she's stressed out. The pair of small pink weights on the sofa look hastily abandoned, and my mom's cheeks are glowing. She reaches for the remote and clicks off the TV without pausing the DVD.

"That's good." Too long has passed since she stopped speaking, but I barrel forward, pretending there was no awkward silence. "It looks good on you."

Mom pushes her hair out of her face and puts her hands on her hips. "Did you just decide to drop by? I can make you something to eat, if you're hungry."

The thought of food turns my stomach, and I give a little laugh. "No, I—I didn't just stop by, but you don't have to drop everything. I'm sorry to interrupt."

She eyes me suspiciously. "What's going on, then? You're usually too busy to show up like this in the middle of the afternoon."

"Oh, I'm busy. I'm really busy." I'm about to be busier, after today. Bernadette's sheer joy at working this deal for me made me realize the best thing I can do is throw myself into Gabriel Luxe instead of wallowing in despair about Jasper. "I just wanted to give you some good news."

Mom narrows her eyes. "What good news? Is this about that young man Evie's been telling me about?"

"Young man? No." She purses her lips. This is coming out all wrong. It's nothing like the big reveal I'd tried to plan on the way here. "I wanted to let you know that I bought this building. You're not going to have to move out. Now, or ever, really, unless you want to."

Her eyes go wide. "You're making some kind of joke."

"I'm not—I got word today that the financing is going through. It'll take another month to close, but—"

My mom jumps into the air, her shriek so shrill I'm surprised the neighbors don't come running. "Isa! Are you serious? Are you *serious*?" She leaps forward, grabbing me by the arms, still hopping. "You did that? You were able to do that?"

"Yes!"

She bursts into tears.

"Mom…" I pat her back as she doubles over.

When she looks back up at me she's beaming. "I'm so proud of you, Isa. You didn't—" She sobs again, but it's almost a laugh. "You didn't have to do this for me. I'm just so amazed—I'm so amazed that you could. I remember all those nights you spent at that sewing machine…" She reaches out and gives me a tight hug, laughing and crying all at the same time.

I laugh, too, but the sound only creates a flicker of warmth in my chest.

It feels hollow.

I won, and it's still hollow.

Still.

CHAPTER FORTY

Jasper

EVERYTHING SEEMS DIFFERENT, NOW THAT THERE'S A GAPING wound in the center of my life that wasn't there last Tuesday.

One week, and the world still looks colorless and dull. That should be impossible, considering I'm in New York City and everything keeps moving around me—cabs pulling up to the curb and speeding away, people stalking down the sidewalks, drivers fighting with each other in the middle of the intersections. I move, too. I get into my town car and back out again. I ride the elevator up to my office and back down. I go to my penthouse.

There's only silence there, and if it's not silent, it's endless reruns of television on Netflix, the sound a river that does its best to block out the endless rehashing of the fight we had, the way elevator shut so definitively behind Isabella when she left.

I can't believe she hasn't texted me.

I can't believe she hasn't called.

I can't believe *I* haven't called.

I could crack up at any moment, but I haven't yet, something that registers in the middle of Tuesday afternoon, when Mike Ford is going through two new potential properties with me.

He points at different lines on the paperwork, taking out the renderings and moving them back as he moves through the options. There are photos, too, taken from outside on the street.

There's a long silence.

Oh. Shit. It's *me* who's supposed to be talking.

"Sorry, Mike. What was the question?"

He leans back in his chair. "What do you think?"

I look back at the papers spread out in front of me. "What's the tenant situation?"

"The final leases would be up in October, and we could move on demolition after that. For this first one, at least. The second one—" He leans forward, choosing one of the pages and twisting it so he can read the numbers. "November."

An image floats up in my mind of Isabella's eyes at that very first meeting, a split second of fear in the middle of her barely contained rage. She wasn't even the one in danger of having to find a new apartment. How many of these people are dying to find a different place to live so that I can make their former homes into luxury condos? Some of them. Maybe. But not all of them. In each of the buildings on the table in front of me, there's going to be some version of Isabella's mother. They definitely won't all have daughters with the brass to confront me about it.

"I don't know, Mike."

He nods, not taking his eyes off me. "I'm happy to look for alternatives."

It's not that I don't want to keep making money for Pace, Inc. I'm damn good at that, and the last thing I'm going to do is give up my career over a bad breakup. But this—the more I look at these buildings, the less I want to move forward.

At least in the same way that we always do.

And when Mike says he'll look for alternatives, I know he means more to choose from, without necessarily discounting these. There's no way I can table every single property he brings me because there are people living in them. It would be a disaster for the business.

"Hey, I'm not trying to stick my nose in your business..." Mike interrupts the silence, which has gotten away from me again. "Are you okay?"

"Yeah." I say it too quickly and I know it. "Yeah, I'm fine. I just—I'll need a minute with these."

"It's almost lunch." Mike sweeps the papers together and puts them back in the folder, pressing it neatly down on the surface of my desk. "I'll stop in later and check in."

I can't help looking past his shoulder. I can just see the corner of Christine's desk outside the door. Isabella walked through that same door, and everything changed. Now she's not going to walk through it again.

"Thanks." But the word lands in the empty air. Mike is already gone.

* * *

"Not straight home tonight, okay?"

Terrence meets my eyes in the rearview mirror. "Where to?"

The names of three different clubs come to mind, but I don't really want to go to any of them. "Hamilton Heights."

He wrinkles his forehead. "Is there a new club there?"

"No. Just someplace I wanted to stop by." I give him the address to the building that was briefly mine, and is now in Isabella's hands. Or at least it will be when the closing finally goes through. I've put all that firmly with the Real Estate department. I told them I didn't want to hear another thing about it. I meant it when I said it. Now I want to go haunt those offices and hover over their shoulders, looking for anything with Isabella's name on it. It's a very attractive quality in a man, to be hovering. Or so I've heard.

I stop paying attention until Terrence pulls up by the curb, the car coming to a gentle stop. "We're here, boss."

"This is it?"

"Yep."

I don't know why I asked. I've been here before, for at least a few minutes. It looks utterly unfamiliar, though.

A burst of laughter next to the door of my car makes me jump back, and I look at the rearview mirror. Terrence isn't focused on me—he's looking out at the people on the sidewalk—so at least he didn't see that embarrassing display.

The woman next to the car laughs again, stepping into view as she moves toward the building. She's petite, with dark hair in a bun at the nape of her neck. The way she moves is achingly familiar.

"...my daughter!" Her voice rises enough for me to hear what she's saying...and the obvious pride in it. If this isn't Isabella's mother, I'll be shocked. My hand goes to the door handle, and I'm on the verge of pushing it open. Before I can, the woman rushes up the stairs to the lobby of the building, a spring in her step, and her friend—a willowy blonde who looks like she's probably in her sixties, continues down the sidewalk, her arms swinging.

I jerk my hand back from the handle.

"We can go." I can't think of any other way to casually get myself the hell away from this building, this heartache. "Back to the penthouse, Terrence."

He gives me a nod in the mirror and pulls the car away from the curb, his hands steady on the wheel.

I curl mine into fists to stop them from shaking.

I have to do something.

I have to.

CHAPTER FORTY-ONE

Isabella

"**E**AT."

Mom puts another serving of lasagna on my plate and goes back for the green beans. I have to force myself not to groan. This is supposed to be celebratory, but I could barely force down the first helping. Even though lasagna was always my favorite when we were growing up. Of course, it was my favorite because Mom only ever made it when something great had happened...like when we made rent six months in a row without a delay or when she landed a slightly better job.

I've been putting this off since last Friday.

I spent the entire weekend wallowing in pajama pants, pretending to get a lot of extra work done in the form of sending copious emails from my phone. I think my couch has a permanent dent in it.

That doesn't matter. I can always get a new couch.

"I'm really—" My mom narrows her eyes at me and adds the green beans over my half-hearted protest. "I don't know if I'll be able to eat all this."

"You're pale, Isa, and you've got huge circles under your eyes." She purses her lips. "I don't think you're taking enough time off."

Evie laughs, taking another bite of lasagna. "Since when has she ever taken time off?"

"I'm taking plenty." In fact, I'm taking too much time off. Too much time during the day, anyway, and then I've been catching up during the nights.

When she brings out the chocolate cake, I feel sick.

I get three bites down before I have to stop, joining in an animated conversation about Evie's upcoming promotion at the fashion house she works for, playing it up as much as I can until my mom finally takes the plates away without another word.

"I wish you could stay longer," she calls from the kitchen.

"I have to get back to the office." I frown for her benefit, just in case she swoops back in while I'm speaking. She doesn't.

"Me too," echoes Evie, and then mom does bustle back in, a plate wrapped up for each of us. My stomach turns over at the thought of eating this again. It might still be my favorite, but I'm not in a celebratory mood. This isn't a good time, and eating it when I feel so shell-shocked—still—feels traitorous. Evie takes her plate, and I take mine with a big smile. I don't think Mom believes it. "I'm really happy for you, Mom."

I give Mom a hug, and then she turns to do the same for Evie. "I wouldn't be here if it weren't for you two."

Evie rolls her eyes, but there's laughter in her expression. "You mean Isa."

"I mean both of you. But yes, your sister did play a big part." Her eyes are shining.

"Don't cry, Mom." I hug her again, then take a deep breath. "I'll see you this weekend, if I can get away."

"See?" She shakes her head, looking at me with a mixture of disapproval and awe. "You don't take enough time off."

"We'll see." Then Evie is dragging me out of the apartment by the elbow.

On the sidewalk, I hang back and let her hail a cab. "You want to share?"

She gives me a look, her flawless black dress flowing in the breeze. "Obviously, Isa. We're going to share. I'm actually going the same place as you are."

My eyebrows draw together. "My office? Why?"

"You'll see."

I don't have the energy to pester her about it on the way back to work. If she wants to come back to my office, that's fine—she can always take another cab, or the train, back to hers.

But Evie doesn't head toward the subway station when we get out of the cab. She presses a tip into the driver's hand and strides toward the entrance of the building, a confident vision in her dress and high heels.

"What are you doing?" I'm still standing by the curb, looking after her like she's the one who's coming slightly unhinged instead of me.

"Going inside. I have a meeting. Are you coming?" Her eyebrows rise above her oversized sunglasses.

"Yep. Yes." I hitch my purse higher up on my shoulder and follow after her.

I don't have to wait long to find out who Evie's meeting is with. She precedes me into my own office, then sits down in one of the seats across from my desk. I'm in my own chair, absently jiggling the mouse to wake up my computer, when Angelique comes in and closes the door tightly behind her. "Hey, Evie."

"Hi, Angelique. How are things?"

"Good." Angelique crosses the office and briskly drops down into the other chair, right next to Evie. Then both of them turn their gazes on me.

"What is this?"

"Why don't you start by telling us?" Evie's voice is calm—too calm.

I glare at her. "Are you staging an intervention?"

"You're driving everyone crazy," says Evie, and Angelique looks at her, daring to nod her head a fraction of an inch.

A wave of anger rises in my chest but dissipates in the face of the emptiness waiting there. "You're driving me crazy. Both of you should get back to work."

"The late nights are becoming a problem, Isa." Angelique

chimes in more tentatively than Evie. "Some of the people on staff are...well, they're at their breaking point. They just can't keep up with you. And during the day..."

"I get it, okay?" I tap the mouse on the desk and the screen finally responds. "I'll be fine by next week. I'll take tomorrow and Friday off, if you think it'll solve the problem."

"I don't." Evie's voice is firm, and her eyes are locked on me. "What's going on with you, Isa? And why didn't you tell me you were feeling like this?"

"I feel fine."

"You're not erratic like this." Evie continues like I never spoke. "You don't force people to be on call at random hours during the night. And you *love* lasagna. You shoved that thing into the mini-fridge like it was chopped liver." She straightens her back. "What's wrong?"

I look from one to the other. They're not baiting me, even if that's what it feels like. They look...concerned. More than concerned. Afraid, even.

What do I have to lose?

"Jasper Pace broke up with me."

Evie rolls her eyes toward the ceiling, then covers her face. "I knew it. I knew you were together. I knew you would be, anyway."

"Well, it's over." I turn fully away from the computer and face them head on. "It's over, so both of you can stop worrying. I'll have myself together by the end of the weekend. That's a promise." I take in a breath. It hurts. "Anything else?"

"I don't think it is over, Isa." Angelique's voice is soft. "I've never seen you like this." She stands up, her hands awkwardly at her sides. Evie follows her lead. "I think you might want to...reconsider. Or at least talk to him."

"For everyone's sake," adds Evie. "But mostly yours."

CHAPTER FORTY-TWO

Jasper

THE PAPERS ARE STARTING TO PILE UP ON MY DESK.

I can't remember the last time things got so out of hand before. I don't think it's actually happened—not to this extent— but every time I pick up one of the packets about potential buildings, my mind spins off onto wild tangents. Isabella's head tilted back, my fingers threaded through her hair. Her eyes flashing that first day in my office. The way her body looks when she's tensed, waiting to come, totally reliant on me. The way she likes to be punished, but only on her terms. The way I could spend an entire afternoon fucking her and still want more at the end.

Everything I do ends in her.

I have to do something about it.

I've known I have to do something about it since Tuesday, when I saw her mother outside that building, beaming with pride and happiness and relief. This is exactly what I was trying to avoid by keeping my focus on work all these years—distractions that will make it less likely for me to make money and more likely for the business to suffer from inattention.

Yet here I am.

How the hell am I supposed to keep developing properties with that same ruthless determination when I'm walking around with a hollow core and zero drive?

I slap the folder in my hand shut again.

"Frustrated?"

My dad stands in the doorway of my office, and I straighten up. "Not in the least. What can I do for you?"

Since the phone call about Isabella, we've been keeping each other at arm's length. I've been relying on an icy professionalism to get through the day, and he's been acting like nothing happened.

"I wanted to talk to you."

"I'm sitting right here." I indicate one of the seats on the other side of my desk, like he's one of my contractors or an investor—someone impersonal and forgettable.

He nods, a strange expression on his face, and steps into the office. He closes the door with a gentle *click* and moves to one of my chairs. When he sits, he does it slowly and carefully. *He's an old man.* He's not the kind of man I would picture in some upscale retirement community in the south of France or somewhere like Florida, but he wouldn't be entirely out of place there.

"I owe you an apology."

I stack up the folders in front of me and snap them against the table, knocking them into a neat row. "For what?"

"I shouldn't have gone behind your back with your girl-friend." The way he says *girlfriend* this time doesn't hold even a hint of malice.

"No, you shouldn't have. But what's done is done."

Dad shifts in his seat, folding his hands in his lap. "I didn't realize how serious things were between you."

I laugh out loud, a short, bitter sound. "We weren't close. We were just..." I search for the right word. "We were just screwing with each other." My dad can't hide the smile that flashes across his face, but he's serious again in an instant. "It was nothing. A fling."

"You were willing to go awfully far for her. That loan..."

"The loan was a stupid idea, and we both know it. I don't need you to remind me."

He puts one hand on the surface of my desk. "I didn't come here to make you feel—" He shakes his head. "I've never known you to even consider doing that for a woman. And you were try-ing to delay the project, and go against me, to save someone close to her. At least, that's what I'm betting."

"Is it my turn to list all the things you shouldn't have done?"

"I think I have a pretty clear idea of what those are. But Jasper..." My dad swallows hard, then looks me in the eye. "You might have learned the wrong lesson from me."

"What lesson?"

"I taught you all the business skills I know." He sighs. "But I didn't teach you that some things are more important than ramming through every project without any regard for the consequences. Things—I should say, some *people* are worth more than that."

"So this was about Mom."

"Son..." He leans back again, squaring his shoulders. "Not much in my life hasn't been about your mother. But I didn't throw myself into this business because I thought loving her wasn't worth it. I did that because even after she...started her affair, I couldn't stop loving her. And sometimes I've been outwardly bitter about that. Sometimes I've said things that make it seem..." He takes a deep breath. "I don't want you to think that no woman will ever be worth your attention. This Ms. Gabriel—she was worth it to you. That's all that matters."

I burst out laughing. "She *played* me."

A twinkle comes to Dad's eye. "And you're telling me that you didn't do the same right back? If I know anything about you, Jasper, you started it."

My throat tightens, but I'll be damned if I cry in front of him. "And what if I did?"

"Then you met your match."

It's a sharp pain my chest, so powerful I almost reach my hand up to try and shove it away. "There's nothing to be done about it now. It's way too late for that."

Dad gives me an indulgent smile. "It's never too late." Then he shrugs. "It might be too late for an old man like me, but not you. I think it's worth another try. If only to get out of this mood." He stands up, smoothing down the front of his jacket. "You're worthless to me if you're dragging down the entire office."

"Message received." He's almost to the office doorway by the time I can speak again. "Dad?"

"Jasper?" He turns back, waiting.

"What the hell am I supposed to do?"

He looks at me for a long moment. It stretches out long enough that I get a flash of him as a young man, obsessed with my mother, excited about the future. He jumped in with both feet with no guarantee that anything would go as planned. And even though it didn't, here he is, trying to convince me to give Isabella another chance. To give the entire mess another chance.

"You do whatever it takes, Jasper. You do whatever it takes."

CHAPTER FORTY-THREE

Isabella

I KEEP ONE PROMISE, AT LEAST—I TAKE THE WEEKEND AND GET myself back together.

Saturday I book myself out completely, morning until night, at a spa and hotel outside the city. There's nothing in it to remind me of Jasper, and nobody there has ever heard of him, so it's a blissful day of being pampered from head to toe. When all of it's finished, I swim laps in the pool, the tiny waves lapping at the tiled edges while the sun sets over the property's manicured lawns.

If he comes into my mind, I let him stay—for a moment. Then I let him go again. I don't linger over thoughts of him. I don't let myself. I'm not going to do that anymore, because it's breaking my damn heart.

Saturday night I settle into the pristine hotel room, where

everything is a blank canvas of whites, splashes of neutral colors the only backdrops for paintings that make me think of absolutely nothing.

Just how I want it.

For the first time since we broke up, I sleep all night.

Sunday morning, I go for another round at the spa's salon. The woman who washes and cuts and dries my hair is the opposite of Celine, my usual hairdresser, who talks a mile a minute and wants to know everything about my life. I'm usually happy to tell her at least some of the details, but this haircut—this haircut is zen.

One more massage, one more lingering shower, and I'm ready to face the city again.

In the car on the way back, the light scent of the spa's soap still clinging to my skin, I watch the traffic surge around us. Cars rush forward, then stop suddenly when the lane backs up. I don't care about any of it. I'm busy cultivating the tiny, *tiny* seed of calm that's blooming slowly in my chest. In the weekend's silence it had a chance to take root, at least.

An airplane hums overhead, leaving a trail of clouds behind it as it heads for the airport.

I could go international.

The thought comes into the new quiet of my brain like a droplet of water on the surface of a pond.

I could expand my online presence, and I could go international with Gabriel Luxe.

This, unlike the calm, is a fast-growing idea, and the moment I start thinking, it's like an explosion of color in my mind.

I could do all of this, and it would eat up every last bit of spare time. It would draw me back into the embrace of sweet, sweet work, and it would keep thoughts of Jasper at bay for long enough for my heart to heal.

Yes, I might need more days at the spa. And yes, I'll still have to make time to decide what to do with my mother's building. But this is the solution.

This is the only good solution.

I spend the rest of Sunday sketching out preliminary ideas, forcing myself to write them down slowly, and carefully, taking time to eat dinner and go for a run. I'll throw myself into it—but while still maintaining enough balance that Angelique and Evie don't feel the need to gang up on me in the middle of the work day.

Is it excitement I feel when I lay down to sleep on Sunday night at a reasonable hour?

It's the shadow of it, at least, and that's enough.

* * *

Monday morning, energy thrums through my veins. I wake up an hour before my alarm and go running in Central Park. I fix my hair and makeup with the kind of focus I haven't been able to grasp since...since things with Jasper took a turn for the worse. But I eat breakfast before I go to the cafe down the block. I'm not going to show up early and start harassing people, even if there's a lot to be done, many plans to hash out.

In fact, I wait until five minutes after I'm supposed to be there to get on the elevator up to the Gabriel Luxe offices.

Angelique is waiting at her desk, and when she sees me, a big smile spreads across her face. "Did you have a nice weekend?"

I know she's really asking *did you talk to him*? I smile back at her. "Very nice. Can you get everybody together in the conference room?"

"Right away." She'll probably also text Evie to tell her that I don't look like a zombie version of myself anymore.

It takes five minutes to get everyone together, and by the time they're all standing in the conference room, eyes on me, I'm ready to get this show on the road.

"Hey, guys." I look out over my team. There's more than one wary expression in the group, and I get it. I really do. "First things first. I owe you an apology." A chorus of denials rings out, and I raise both hands in the air to bring it to an end. "I do. I've been... going through a hard time recently, but I'm happy to say that I'm on the other side and I'm ready to go back to business as usual."

Someone in the back starts clapping, and I can't help laughing as the applause swells toward the front of the room.

"Thank you. But I wouldn't have been able to do it without a few of you setting me straight." I take a deep breath. "You should also know that over the weekend I came up with some new plans for Gabriel Luxe."

The tension grows in the room for one heartbeat, then two, and finally Angelique is the one to break the silence. "Well, don't leave us in suspense! God, Isa!"

"Sorry! Sorry. I was just—" I shake my head. "Here's what I want to do next. I want to expand our presence overseas. New York State isn't enough for me, and I know it's not enough for you, either." Cheers and whoops rise over the group. "And while plans are proceeding nicely on the new storefronts—they should be operational within the next six weeks—I don't think we're doing enough online."

"Will this mean hiring more staff?" It's a guy named Dan, calling out from the back.

"Yes."

"Thank God!" Everyone laughs.

"I'm going to need all of you to make Gabriel Luxe bigger and better, but I want to promise you right now that even if things get crazy, it'll be because the business needs our attention, not because I don't know when to quit. Are you with me?"

This time, they clap even harder. When the meeting breaks up, everybody riding the high of a new beginning, Dan is the first to come up to me and ask about raises.

I laugh. "I'll look at that first thing," I tell him. "We're taking this one step at a time."

I'm already one step away from the despair that's hounded me all this time. One more step. I just need one more step...

CHAPTER FORTY-FOUR

Jasper

I F I LOOK AT THESE PROPERTY DETAILS ONE MORE TIME, I'M going to drive myself insane.

But I can't put them down.

The solution is here, right in front of me, but I can't see it.

I lean back in my desk chair and rub my eyes. What time is it? I've been sitting here since everybody else went home. It can't have been more than a couple of hours ago, only—shit, the sun is set. It's dark outside. Well, it's as dark outside as it ever gets in New York City, with the ambient light from all the buildings and cars and streetlights glowing in an orange haze above the skyline. I pick up my phone from the desk.

It's one a.m.

I can't leave here until I figure out what to do.

The weekend was excruciatingly long, every hour stretching

out into three or four. I don't want to leave the penthouse, but halfway through Saturday afternoon, Dominic Wilder texted me and insisted on a night out.

You can't spend forever holed up in your penthouse.

I'd paused the show I was watching without taking any of it in.

How the hell do you know what I do with my spare time?

New York's not that big a place.

It's big enough for you to leave me alone, isn't it?

Not a chance. Come out tonight. Vivienne insists.

I leaned my head back against the armrest of the couch. New York City is only so small if your circle of friends is limited to the people who work in your office and a group of other nosy people with enough money to buy the time to care if one of their own hasn't been seen in public for a couple of weeks.

So I went.

Vivienne's eyes sparkled when she saw me. "Where's your lady friend?"

"I don't have a lady friend."

Her expression fell in disappointment. "I liked her. What happened?"

I'd clutched at my chest like the pain was too much to bear. "You hardly knew her. And anyway, it wasn't serious."

She narrowed her eyes at me. "It wasn't? It looked pretty serious at the restaurant opening."

"Looks can be deceiving."

"Is it deceiving that you look kind of sickly and pale and you haven't been out in way too long?"

"What are you, some kind of surveillance officer?"

"I notice things."

"I notice that I don't have a drink."

"First round's on me." Dominic slapped his hand on the table and called for the waiter. "Cheer up, Jasper. It's not the end of the world, whatever it is." Then he cocked his head to the side, reconsidering. "Although if it *is* the end of the world, you should either get her back or move on."

Vivienne gave him a smile that crackled with heat, then turned her gaze on me. "Dominic chose door number one."

"I'm *so* happy for you guys." We all laughed.

For the rest of the night I tried to keep my head in the conversation, but I couldn't ignore the deluge of ideas rushing through my brain. None of them seemed like they were worth pursuing. None of them seemed worthy of Isabella, anyway.

Sunday went by in the same fashion, then Monday.

By this morning, I'd lost count of the number of coffees and energy drinks I'd poured into my body, trying to use every last moment to figure out what to do.

Whatever it takes.

My dad's words keep ringing in my ears, but could he have been any vaguer? It's not like he dropped everything and tried to get my mother back. It's not like she would have come back even if he had. But *whatever it takes* doesn't narrow down the options.

I look through the papers one more time. This situation with the buildings—it's separate from Isabella. Figuring out what to do with the buildings won't tell me what to do for her. Am I seriously going to be left with groveling at her doorstep, nothing in hand?

No. I can't do that.

Screw that.

Two of the buildings Mike brought for my consideration are next to each other, a sidewalk between them, leading back to an alley. The sidewalk is a literal middle ground. If we went forward with those, it would need some landscaping, and we'd have to work with the city on—

A middle ground.

The phrase rattles around in my mind, again and again. Middle ground. Middle ground.

There's a middle ground between the buildings.

There's a middle ground between gutting everything and keeping some of it.

There's a middle ground between forcing out all the original tenants and installing new ones who can afford to pay the high prices I'm going to charge.

But I don't have to charge those prices for every single unit.

No.

In fact, I could reconfigure the units entirely so that the luxury condos are up near the top of the building, with separate access to some of the amenities. I could improve the buildings overall while still leaving space for some of the tenants who don't want to leave. As they gradually move out, I can convert the spaces into more condos...or even leave a few units in each building separate.

They wouldn't be on the luxury level, but...

It's going to lose money.

That's a truth I can't deny, and it might be a hard sell to some of the people we're selling the condos to, but I'm confident I can pull it off. And the PR boost would be incredible. It might even shake loose my reputation for being such a heartless bastard.

I open the folder with a flutter of papers. We're not going to keep every building and rent out the space. Some of them, we can still develop the way Pace, Inc. always has—a total renovation from the inside out. But others...

Others could be different.

Alongside all of this, a new idea is forming in the back of my mind. Isabella isn't a real estate developer, and now she's got an aging building on her hands. Is she really going to leverage Gabriel Luxe's resources to get a handle on it?

If I can pull this off, she might not have to.

And even if it's not enough to show her how I feel about her, still, after all the terrible things we both said...

My throat goes tight.

I'm not going to think about that right now.

Instead, I pick up the folders, tuck them into my briefcase, and head for the door. I have to get some sleep. And then I have to get on the phone.

My heart beats furiously on the way to the car in a silent prayer.

Please, let this work.

CHAPTER FORTY-FIVE

Isabella

ANGELIQUE STICKS HER HEAD IN THE DOORWAY OF MY OFFICE. "You doing okay? Need another cup of coffee?"

I pretend to shake from the caffeine jitters. "I don't know. Think I should have one?"

She rolls her eyes. "I'm sending one of the interns out."

"In that case, *yes*. I do. The fanciest one money can buy."

Angelique laughs on the way back to her desk, and I hear her ordering the drinks over the phone. Then she's back at the door. "Anything else?"

"No, I'm good."

"Okay." She looks down at her watch. "You've got a meeting in five with the new website developer, and one in forty-five with the business manager to talk about building your international presence." Angelique's eyes are serious when she looks back up at me. "Do you want me to move anything around? Need a break?"

"Stop hovering. I'm fine."

"You've been working like a madwoman."

"Angelique." I give her a stern look. "I have been leaving by six o'clock every day. I spend an hour exercising every morning. I bought health food for my apartment. How much more do you want from me?"

"I just want to make sure you're not cracking up. Isn't this all a little much?"

"Do you think it's a little much?"

"I think *you're* a little much to begin with." We both laugh. "I just—you know, I worry about you. Plus, I've got Evie checking in every other day."

"She's just as much of a workaholic."

Angelique shrugs, pretending to tear up. "We just—we just love you, Isa."

"I know. Now get out of my office."

My coffee arrives in the middle of the meeting with the web developer. The first sip almost derails the entire thing—it's that good. "I'm sorry. I'm *so* sorry," I say to him. "Angelique?"

Angelique is at the door in an instant. "What's up?"

"Make a note that this—whatever this is—is my new favorite drink of all time." It's blended and involves caramel and whipped cream. I want one every day until things have settled down at Gabriel Luxe, which could be never.

The thought of that makes me nervous. If all of my new plans keep rolling forward with this much momentum, I might never have time to fall for a man again.

Isn't that the point, though?

I snap myself out of it just in time. "Thanks, Angelique." I look back at Brian who's got a forgiving grin on his face. "Tell me more about ecommerce platforms. We've got a simple one right now, but the orders there aren't nearly what I'd like them to be."

He leans forward, swiping across the screen of the tablet he brought in with a mockup already created. "Well, there's the platform, and then there's the marketing. It looks like you haven't done much aggressive online marketing, and it's going to be a different animal from the print advertising you've relied on so far."

"I'm going to need a separate team for all this. Right?"

He nods. "Probably more than one. If your site takes off, you might even need upgraded production facilities to handle the demand." Then he smiles at me. "Of course, if you hire me to work with your existing web team, the site *will* take off."

Brian is attractive. He has a nice smile, and had he waltzed into my office six weeks ago, I might have had a little crush on him. But his blue eyes just make me think of Jasper. My heart twists in my chest. *Damn it...*

I let the thought of Jasper come and go like it's on a peaceful ocean wave, or whatever bullshit my meditation app has been telling me to do lately.

Then I move on to the other meetings.

It's after lunch when Bernadette knocks at my door. I'm still stabbing at the salad Angelique insisted on bringing me. It's good, but so gigantic I'm having trouble forcing myself through the lettuce. Bernadette is the perfect excuse to stop eating it.

"Thank God you're here. I was getting sick of this salad's company."

She laughs, then takes her seat across the desk from me. "Have you—have you thought at all about what you'd like to do with the Hamilton Heights building?"

"Leave it how it is."

Bernadette nods, looking off to the side. "I see."

I fold my hands on the surface of the desk. "Bernadette, what is it that you're not telling me?"

She looks back at me, pursing her lips like she can't decide whether to reveal her life's deepest secret or not. "Leaving the building as is—that's one option. But we're going to need to look into renovations if you're going to continue keeping tenants there." Her eyebrows draw together. "There's a lot that goes into this, Isa, and I'm not sure we're equipped to handle it through Gabriel Luxe."

"I'll handle it through my personal budget, then. That's not a problem." I give her a pointed look. "Why is this on your mind? We've moved on to other things for the time being."

"Well..." She trails off, eyes searching my face for—for I don't know what. Some kind of clue, I guess, but she doesn't find what she's looking for. Instead, she squares her shoulders and takes a deep breath.

"Bernie, what the hell is wrong with you? Not to be too blunt."

"I've had a call from a...potential investor."

"An investor in the building?" That makes approximately zero sense. There's not really anyone who knows I've purchased it, unless Pace, Inc. puts out a press release every time they sell a building to a desperate woman. All I know about the building is that I want my mom to be able to keep living there. I didn't plan to make a killing off of it. I vaguely had a plan to put one of my storefronts on the ground floor, and maybe some kind of branded fitness studio. I had more of a plan at one point, but now I'm starting over.

At any rate, there are only a few people who knew about the purchase and would have any interest in pursuing investment. The moment I figure that out, my heart sinks.

Bernadette is still looking at me with the world's most cautious expression. "Yes. An investor in the building."

"Who is it, Bernadette?"

"That's the thing."

I feel like I'm tumbling over the edge of a cliff. "What did you do?"

She looks at me and bites her lip. "It's not that I—"

"Did you ask him to come here?"

"No. He—" She shakes her head. "He just showed up. He's waiting in the lobby."

CHAPTER FORTY-SIX

Jasper

I T'S A DAMN HARD THING, TO STARE AT AN ELEVATOR, UNABLE TO tear your eyes away from the silver doors, while also pretending you don't care at all about who steps out of them.

Only I *do* care. I care so much that after ten minutes I give in, take a seat on one of the benches in the building's lobby, and stare.

It's not the image I like to project of myself—some lovelorn, pathetic man staring at an elevator—but there's nobody I recognize in the lobby. I'll still be able to maintain my reputation as one of New York's most powerful businessmen after this potentially mortifying trip to the Gabriel Luxe offices.

I hope.

At least I'm not sitting in the actual offices, which is perhaps the only saving grace of the entire situation.

The woman I talked to on the phone, Bernadette, did not sound enthusiastic about taking my message to Isabella. I explained who I was in the interest of honesty. This isn't a game anymore, and I didn't want to start this off with some kind of deception to get the love of my life—because that's what she is, the damn *love of my life*—down to the lobby to have a conversation with me. I wanted it to be on her terms.

I regret that more and more with every minute that goes by.

I called the Gabriel Luxe offices the moment they opened for business, looking for the person mostly likely to handle investors and other kinds of projects like the one I'm about to propose, and got Bernadette. Of course, that doesn't mean Isabella was ready to take a meeting with her as soon as I hung up. I waited as long as I could before I came here, anyway. It's well past lunch. That doesn't really mean anything. She could still be busy. Isabella is usually busy, but Bernadette did say she would be in during the afternoon, so...

The elevator doors slide open, and my heart crashes against my ribs.

Two silver-haired men step out, talking heatedly about a baseball team.

My shoulders sag at the sight of them.

The doors close again, and the elevator goes back up.

I have no idea if she's going to come down or not. And if she does...

The doors open again, the gentle ding taking over my entire life. I flick my eyes toward it, not daring to hope.

Isabella steps out into the lobby.

Her mouth is pressed into a thin, nervous line, and her eyebrows are drawn together. My entire chest aches at the sight of her, looking for me, scanning the space with her arms crossed over her chest, like she might need to ward off an attack.

I stand up, and the movement catches her eye.

There's a flicker of a smile on her face.

It gives me just enough hope to force myself into movement, to cross the lobby, and to stand next to her. The scent of her in the air, clean and familiar and lovely, is almost too much to bear.

Isabella takes a breath in and opens her mouth, but no words come out. Not for a moment, at least. "I'm supposed to be meeting with a potential investor."

I laugh, and some of the tension in my chest breaks apart. Isabella looks like she might consider smiling if everything goes exactly right, but something in the way she holds herself relaxes. A little. "That would be me."

Another breath through her nose. "What are you hoping to invest in, Jasper?"

My name on her tongue is the sliver of an invitation. She could have said *you horrible man* or *you prick*, but she went with my name. I have to believe that this is a good sign. "Would you like to come somewhere with me?"

She raises her eyebrows. "Right now?"

I think of her marching into my office, not taking no for an answer. I think of her eyes flashing with anger and confidence. The Isabella who walked into my life that day would consider it, then tell me to screw off. She only ever goes anywhere if she's decided on it herself.

"Unless you'd rather...meet up another time. Or not at all." It's a risk, throwing that last option out there. She might just take it.

Instead, she waits, her gaze flicking down to the floor and then back up at my eyes. "I don't have a lot of time. I'm very busy."

"It won't take much of your time."

She nods her head toward the elevator. "You're sure you wouldn't rather come sit in my office? I'm sure I'll be able to give you a yes or no fairly quickly."

It's too businesslike, the tone of her voice, but there's a tremble underneath that tells me this is no business dealing. Not for her. She hasn't moved on yet. At least, that's what I'm hoping. Desperately.

"There's something I'd like to show you."

Isabella squares her shoulders, drawing herself up to her full height. "I'm not sure that I should go anywhere with you." Her voice is oddly formal, but I catch the quiver in her lip that she tries to hide, and there's a strain in her tone that drives home how hard it is for her to even be standing with me.

"No, you shouldn't." I lower my voice so that the words are

for her, and her only. "You shouldn't, because I hurt you. And I know that. The things I said to you were—" I have to look away from her, but I force my gaze back to her eyes. "You're well within your rights to never forgive me. If you want to walk away right now, I won't stop you."

"You came all this way willing to be humiliated in the lobby of my building?" She's trying her best to lighten the unbearable heaviness of all this, and my heart breaks all over again.

"I'm hoping it won't come to that." I give her a tentative smile. "But yes."

Isabella sighs, making a show of glancing down at her watch. "I'll give you half an hour."

CHAPTER FORTY-SEVEN

Isabella

Nothing feels more normal—and more terrifying— than climbing into the back of Jasper's town car with him.

He keeps his distance, not making a single move toward me. I can hardly stand it. I want to throw myself into his arms, but at the same time, I'm worried that if he touches me, it will be all over. I'm busy moving on. I'm busy with Gabriel Luxe. I don't need to get sucked back into this vicious, selfish love for him.

I just might not be able to help it.

This is probably a mistake, but the part of me that cares has been shouted down by the part of me that just wants to be with him. Near him. In sight of him, even.

"What is it that you wanted to show me?"

"You'll see." A smile quirks at the corner of his mouth.

My throat aches, a sob rising even though he's said hardly anything since the town car pulled away from the curb. "Jasper—"

"Yes?" He turns toward me, away from the window, his blue eyes searching mine.

"I'm—I'm sorry for what I said, too."

He nods. "You had every right to be upset."

"It upset me because it was true, what you said."

Jasper lets out a short burst of laughter. "You are *not* a gold-digging bitch."

"But I did use you."

"Sometimes people do stupid things. I'm the one who challenged you to do it in the first place. I should never have bought that building."

"Because my mother lives there?"

"Because *people* live there. I was...grossly misled by the seller, and someone on my team slipped up on those leases. Ultimately, that's on me."

An iced-over section of my heart warms and cracks. Jasper Pace, telling me that he cares about the people who live in the buildings he buys? Who *is* this guy?

He catches me staring. "What?"

"Did something happen to you while we were—while we weren't talking?"

"Why do you ask?"

"Because the Jasper Pace I know would never—" A giggle

bubbles up in my chest. "Well, the Jasper Pace I thought I knew would never have given a shit whether one of his buildings still had tenants in it or not."

"You're wrong about that. There are laws." His eyes dance in the sunlight, but then his expression turns serious. "There are laws, but something did happen to me that made me realize that...it's not always worth it. Brushing people aside isn't, I mean."

"What happened?"

He gives me a long, level look. "You."

It's all I can do not to launch myself across the seat at him, to rip off his jacket, to tear open his shirt. Part of that has to do with the words coming out of his mouth, but most of it has to do with the close proximity of the back of the town car, the way my body has been aching for him so relentlessly that it wakes me up in the middle of the night, the way he infiltrates my dreams, even when I'm determined not to think of him.

More than that, I want to be totally surrounded by his arms, all the heat in the world contained in our embrace. It sounds stupid. It probably is stupid. But it's what I want.

I'm beginning to think...

No.

I can't even start to hope.

Terrence pulls the car to a stop next to the curb, and Jasper opens the door and climbs out, offering his hand to me. We're exactly where I thought we were going. I recognized the way almost immediately.

"What are we doing here?"

Jasper looks up at my mother's building, all five floors of it, shading his eyes from the sun with his hand. He stares at it for a long moment, and then he looks back into my eyes. The silver in his eyes catches the light and reflects it back. It takes my breath away.

He presses his mouth into a hard line, then seems to make a decision.

He reaches out and takes my hand.

The moment he touches me, my body sags with relief—so much so that my knees start to buckle. Jasper sweeps one arm around my waist, catching me before I tumble onto the sidewalk. Heat rushes to my cheeks. "God, this is—" I laugh, using him to stand upright and brush the invisible embarrassment off my skirt suit. "This is embarrassing."

"I'll take the attention off of you." He turns us both so that we're facing the building. "This building was just one of many that I was looking to buy and gut and profit from in New York City, but you changed that, Isabella."

It doesn't look like much, but when I glance up at my mother's window, tears come to my eyes. It doesn't look like much but it means everything.

"This building brought you into my office." He takes my other hand in his, turning me back toward him. "This building is the reason you swept into my life like a storm and rearranged the whole thing. Only with you, I'm better than I was before. You made me see—" He swallows hard. "You made me see that a business can only take you so far. If you want to go beyond that, you need...you need humanity. You need love." He takes one more deep breath. "I'm sorry I called you a gold-digging bitch. I'm sorry I accused you of fucking around with me. I think we both know that it only started out that way. And even if you don't feel the same way about me, I had to bring you here, to show you that—"

I cut him off.

I have to.

I can't wait another moment.

I throw my arms around his neck and leap up, wrapping my legs around his waist, kissing him hard.

It's like the first taste of water after a year in the desert. It's like the first breath of warmth after a year in the snow. Kissing Jasper, hard and hot and without a shred of restraint, makes my heart burst open. The words spill from my lips between kisses. "I love you. I *love* you. Every day without you was like a thousand fucking years."

He laughs, holding me tightly to him, lifting me as if I were weightless. For the moment, maybe I am.

It's a long time before he sets my feet back on the sidewalk.

"I love you, Isabella."

I try three times to catch my breath, and finally I'm able to speak again. "I love you." I look back into his gorgeous, soul-shattering blue eyes. "Now, tell me about this investment idea you had."

CHAPTER FORTY-EIGHT

Jasper

I LAUGH OUT LOUD, A LIGHT, GIDDY FEELING WELLING UP IN MY chest. "I want to know something first."

"What?"

"Are you going to be mine? And not in some fucked-up deal where it lasts for less than a month and then we both screw it up."

"I don't know. I want to know about this supposed investment." Isabella's green eyes are shining in the afternoon sun, and I want nothing more than to take her back to my penthouse and pick up where we left off. I grin at her. Not agreeing to a damn thing before she hears all the details? That's my girl.

I turn back to the building. "I know you—or at least Gabriel Luxe—own this property now, but I'm assuming you don't have the people on staff to develop it like it deserves."

"Oh, no." She's already shaking her head. "I am *not* going to tear out everything charming about this building and make the people here—"

"That's not what I'm suggesting."

Isabella narrows her eyes. "What *are* you suggesting, then?"

"I'm not going to take this over. Not a chance of that. This project is in your hands now. I just thought you might like a little help. Maybe to share some of my...resources."

She glances back up at the building, taking it in again. Maybe this time she's seeing the repair work that needs to be done on the front facade, the way the staircase could be enhanced and made accessible, and how the lobby could be refreshed, the storefronts on the bottom floor reconfigured and revitalized so that they're not quite so run down. "To do what, exactly?"

"I imagine you're not into luxury condos."

"Not really, no."

"Not any?"

"Cut to the chase, Jasper. I'm a busy woman." She says it with a smile so brilliant it makes the sun seem dark.

"What about two, on the top floor?"

"You'd want to put luxury condos on the top floor of a building with no elevator?"

"I'd have the elevator added."

"Two condos—and the rest?"

"Rent-controlled apartments."

Isabella laughs out loud. "You're kidding. That wouldn't make any money."

"Is profit an issue for you?"

She shrugs, but her eyes travel over the front of the building again. "Not the only issue. The main issue for me is fairness. Some of the people who've lived here—" Her mouth turns downward into a determined frown. "I'm not going to throw them out, or jack up the prices and force them to leave."

"But you're still going to need to make money on the building."

Isabella sighs. "Yes. In the long run, yes."

"Then here's my plan." I step behind her and point at the building, starting at the top. "Those two units become luxury condos with their own amenities. This neighborhood is up-and-coming, and there will be people dying for a quirky apartment with all the nice things they've come to expect." Isabella presses her body back against mine, the heat between us building. "Below that, three floors of affordable apartments."

"How affordable?"

My cock is hard at her touch. She has to feel it. "Affordable enough for your mother to stay without worrying. Down the line, as people move out, we can convert the rest into condos, or leave them as is. Or have a combination. Either way, I'm confident I can sell it."

She wriggles her ass back against me, just a little bit, just to torture me.

"And on the bottom floor, you could—" I suck in a breath, try not to get carried away in the middle of the sidewalk. "You could put in a Gabriel Luxe store, and a restaurant. Anything else you wanted, really. You could just refurbish the building and let the tenants who are here now have first pick. If you wanted."

"Why so breathless, Jasper?" Isabella's voice is teasing, light, and I love every word out of her mouth. I love it. I love her.

"I'm having a bit of an issue."

"What issue is that?"

"That we're in public instead of my penthouse."

"Why didn't you say something?" Isabella turns in my arms, rising on her tiptoes to kiss the line of my jaw, her lips leaving a hot imprint behind. "We could have left minutes ago."

Isabella rides me hard and fast, her hands braced against my chest, my fingers sinking into her hips. She's a sight to behold, her hair spilling down her shoulders, her head thrown back, lips parted. Her face is pink from multiple orgasms, and her nipples are hard little pebbles against the swell of her breasts.

I reach up with one hand and roll one between my fingers, making her gasp.

I don't know how many times she's come so far, but she's going to do it one more time if it's the last thing I do.

I reach forward and trace my thumb down her navel as she rises up and down, the tight, wet core of her enveloping every inch of my shaft. She's almost there—I can feel it in the way she trembles, in the way her pussy clenches around me—and all it's going to take...*all* it's going to take...

My thumb makes contact with her clit.

Isabella arches her back, a low cry escaping her as she comes, thrusting herself down onto my cock, her hips circling and bucking, all of her tensing and releasing. I can't resist any longer. I come so hard my vision goes dark at the edges. All I can see is her. It's all I need to see.

When she's finished, she tumbles sideways onto the comforter of my bed, curling up next to me. Her breathing settles in, and then she lets out a soft sigh.

"You don't have to do this for me," she says.

"Do what?"

"Help me...repair my mom's building."

"It's not just a plan for her building."

She props herself up on one elbow. "No?"

"No. I'm already making plans at Pace, Inc. to follow that format in at least a quarter of the new buildings we develop from now on. Maybe more."

Isabella's eyes dance. "You're going to let people stay in their homes?"

I look into those green eyes and fall for her all over again. It must be the hundredth time today. "Only if you promise not to call me a heartless bastard."

She laughs. "Only if you promise not to let me forget that I love you, even when we fight."

I flutter my eyelashes at her. "How could you ever forget that?"

"I couldn't." She leans down and kisses me, and this time it's full of all the softness and tenderness I could ever want.

"How could I make people move away from home…" I murmur the words when she pulls back and rests her head against my chest. "…when I'll never have to leave mine, as long as you're with me?"

Isabella looks up at me, and there's nothing but love shining from her eyes. "I'm not going anywhere."

Then she reaches for me again, and there are no more words left to say.

EPILOGUE

Isabella, six months later

"**Y**OU HAVE TO EAT, OTHERWISE YOU'LL WASTE AWAY!"

Mom dishes another serving of cheesecake onto Jasper's plate. She spent all week perfecting the recipe, and I don't think she's ever been prouder of anything in her life.

He doesn't even try to turn her down. "I don't think wasting away will be a problem." Everyone around the table laughs, Evie loudest of all.

She turns to me. "You didn't tell me he was funny."

I roll my eyes. "He's been to dinner at least five times already. You know how funny he is." She knows how funny his dad can be, too—she insisted on meeting him at the second dinner. They have a lot in common, Jasper and his father.

My mom takes her seat at the table and watches Jasper eat the second slice of cheesecake with more than a little bit of adoration in her eyes. Midway through, she winks at me. It's not very well hidden, but Jasper just smiles.

When he's finished, he waits for Evie to finish telling us about the latest workplace drama at her fashion house, and then he turns to my mother. "The renovations haven't been bothering you too much, have they?"

Contractors started work on the top floor of the building last month. The exterior work won't be started until the spring—at least, that's what I understand.

She beams at Jasper. "Oh, no. They're very quiet. And they keep such strict hours. I've never been kept awake."

He frowns a little. "Hmm."

She leans toward him, instantly worried. "Was that—are they supposed to be bothersome?"

Jasper can't keep a straight face. "I'm sorry. No, they're not. But I was thinking..." He taps the side of his cheek. I have to force myself not to roll my eyes, but I can't keep the smile off my face, either. This playful side of him...I could get used to this.

"What? What were you thinking?" My mom fiddles anxiously with the tablecloth, and Evie sits beside her, grinning like she's already in on the secret.

"I was thinking that if you were bothered by the construction efforts, I might be able to help."

"Well, how? I would never want to inconvenience you..."

"I have some property in the south of France that I've been

meaning to visit for quite some time. I was actually planning to leave in two weeks."

Mom's forehead wrinkles. She's not getting it, but Evie is.

She can't contain herself. "Jasper, are you inviting us all to visit your villa in the south of France?"

He snaps his fingers like it's the best idea he's ever heard. "That's exactly what I'm doing. You, and my father will be there too. It will be a wonderful…family vacation."

"*What?*" My mom leaps up from her seat. "France? In two weeks?"

"It's for real, Mom." I have to shout the words over the burst of applause she's giving Jasper. "You can come, too, can't you, Evie?"

"Um, *yes.* Yes. I will do whatever it takes. How long are we staying?"

"At least two weeks." Jasper looks at me. "There are lots of things I'd like to do there."

My entire body hums with anticipation. Jasper hasn't said anything yet, but in all the discussions we've had about engagements and weddings, I've always been sure to mention that I want my mom to be there. She's been there for everything else.

"Pack your bathing suits!" I cry, and my mom scrambles away from the table, toward her bedroom. "Where are you going?" I call after her.

"Shopping!" She shouts the word from her bedroom, then

reemerges with her purse over her shoulder and her coat already half-on. "Come with me!" Mom rushes for the door. "Oh, I've never been so excited in my life!"

I lean in and kiss Jasper, the heat spreading through my entire core.

Outside my mother's apartment, he takes me by the elbow and pulls me in for another kiss before we climb into the town car.

"There's something I wanted to ask you." His voice is a low murmur, and it makes me think of all the things we're going to do the moment we get back to the penthouse.

"Anything."

"If I ask you to marry me in France, will you say yes?"

My smile is so wide it almost hurts. "Are you worried I might say no?"

"I'm sure it's what you want. But I still wanted to ask." He slides his arm around my waist, holding me tight, like he'll never let go. "Just in case there are already plans for a wedding." His eyes are shining, and he leans down to whisper in my ear. "I can't wait to be married to you. Two weeks is almost too long. Is that something you want, too?"

My family by my side. An engagement *and* a wedding in the south of France. Being Jasper's wife, without another delay. My heart is consumed with joy.

"Oh, I do," I tell him, rising on tiptoes to press my lips against his. "I *do*."

For more books by Amelia Wilde, visit her online at

awilderomance.com.

Made in the USA
Las Vegas, NV
12 September 2021